SISTERS OF DREAMS AND REDEMPTION

BY VLADARG DELSAT

2024

Copyright © 2024 by **Vladarg Delsat**

All rights reserved.

No part of this publication may be reproduced, distributed, or transmitted in any form or by any means, including photocopying, recording, or other electronic or mechanical methods, without the prior written permission of the publisher, except as permitted by copyright law.

The story, all names, characters, and incidents portrayed in this production are fictitious. No identification with actual persons (living or deceased), places, buildings, and products is intended or should be inferred.

Book Cover by **Izabela Novoselec**

Edited by **Geraldine Nyika**

PRAISE FOR VLADARG DELSAT

Sisters of Dreams and Redemption is a YA mystery/thriller that explores themes of transformation and forgiveness. Masha's journey from a troubled past to an uncertain future is both heartbreaking and inspiring. What struck me most about this book was its emotional depth and the way it navigates complex family dynamics with sensitivity. It's a story that stays with you, reminding us of the power of resilience and the possibility of redemption even in the darkest of times.

AIGAIL L, LIBRARIAN

Hold onto your hats, readers! Sisters of Dreams and Redemption isn't your average YA mystery—it's a rollercoaster of emotions! Imagine a tale where fate and forgiveness collide in the most unexpected ways. Masha's journey from tormentor to tormented is a whirlwind of secrets and surprises. This book will tug at your heartstrings and keep you guessing until the very end. Discover why it's a great read for anyone craving a story that's as transformative as it is thrilling

SUE E., REVIEWER

CONTENTS

Introduction	vii
Bully	1
Evil begets evil	11
Orphan	19
Hospice	29
The ghost of salvation	39
Hospital	47
Sisters-in-dream	57
The sea	65
The dreaded black sorcerer	73
Who loves tears	83
Accident	93
A stroke of fate	105
Orphanage	115
School for Disabled Children	125
Ded Moroz and the chance	135
Salvation	145
Mummy, Daddy and Alyona	155
Embassy	165
Error management	175
Somewhere far away	185
New Year	195
A present from Ded Moroz	205
Welcome to the school	215
Flow of time	225

INTRODUCTION

Greetings, reader,

and welcome to an adventure through a harsh and sensitive reality situated within the vast and mysterious borders of Russia. This story, which is based on true events that happened no more than 20 years ago, transports you to a place where it's difficult to distinguish between the human spirit's capacity for perseverance and harsh reality.

You will meet some incredible people in these pages who have gone through some very difficult times. You'll learn about instances of bullying that have been so severe that the victims have nearly died, and you'll witness how society has disregarded or forgotten some of its own members. In Russia, living with a disability involves more than just getting around. It's about being handled as though you've passed away already.

Despite these terrible depictions, the resiliency of the human spirit appears. In this terrible setting, fairy tale figures find their home, shedding light on the darkest parts of human existence. These stories are about more than just survival; they show how, even in the most terrible situations, there is room for hope and transformation.

This book invites readers to go past the surface of cultural expectations and into the profound difficulties and accomplishments of those who live in the shadows of existence. Everything you are about to read may have occurred. In fact, most of it did! What unfolds is a monument to the enormous fortitude and perseverance it takes to negotiate such a environment, as well as the guts to share.

Prepare to be affected, disturbed, and ultimately changed by what awaits!

BULLY

ELDER

"Take it, you bitch!" I punch her in the stomach to worsen the pain in her leg. Lerka, daring to speak out without permission, collapses onto the filthy floor, huddling in a lump. She anticipates my next move, knowing I'll kick her leg to put her in her place, the scum. The girls around us goad me on with their shouts, and I quickly grab the belt from my bag, striking her wherever I can reach. Despite Lerka's screams, no one intervenes, not even the teachers, who seem indifferent.

I feel a sense of superiority, knowing that even the boys wouldn't dare challenge me. My anger is quick to ignite, and those who provoke it will regret their actions. Lerka, typically reserved, seemed to break from her usual demeanor today, resulting in her receiving punishment with the belt. Perhaps this method will be useful for handling others in the future.

"Turn her over!" I command, and the girls immediately comply, understanding my intentions as I proceed to punish Lerka relentlessly until exhaustion sets in. Everyone here follows my lead, with some even finding enjoyment in it. Von Lariska takes pleasure in witnessing the humiliation of others, while Tanka revels in their screams and pleas. Lerka will now be forced to lick Tanka's shoes, but I've already vented my frustrations and no longer find it interesting.

In truth, I'm not simply bullying Lerka; rather, today she let her guard down and must learn to keep her mouth shut. She won't dare speak up out of fear, and my parents will protect me anyway, while the other girls will deny any wrongdoing. If there's any trouble, Lerka knows she'll have to deal with it herself. Such dynamics are the norm in this school.

I wash my hands after the ordeal, hearing the sounds of whimpering and sobbing behind me as Tanka continues her program of punishment. It's time for me to leave and head home. Lerka will remember this experience, serving as a lesson to others—when I speak, everyone listens.

Exiting the restroom, I instinctively lash out at a student from another class who mistakenly lingered nearby. Violence is a possibility here, but others know better than to provoke me; they understand the consequences. It's a jungle-like environment, but if I don't assert myself, I'll be relegated to a lower status, just as I was in the first grade. I've learned my lesson since then and now make sure to assert my dominance whenever necessary.

I slip on my jacket and glance around before making my way out of the school toward the bus stop. The frantic kid I kicked doesn't even cross my mind; he'll be fine, the wide-eyed fool. He shouldn't have been lurking near the restroom anyway. Oh, there's my bus.

My ancestors are pretty ordinary, as ordinary as these old folks who don't seem to know how to live properly. I should at least run a comb through my hair to avoid getting itchy ears. "You're acting like a girl." So what if I am? Guys hit girls all the time, and grope them, and... worse. If you don't fight back, they'll corner you in a stall and... well, you get the idea. Everyone's aware of it, but how... Well, so far, it hasn't happened to me. And if it does, who's going to say anything? Even though the guys seem reasonable enough, there's a big difference between undressing and crossing that line.

They say there's a new girl joining us tomorrow. Either she's sick or she's crazy, and that's probably why they warned me not to lay a finger on her today. Mihalna, our head teacher, tried to show sympathy and singled her out. Long story short, the new girl's got a target on her back; she might as well stop breathing. We'll need to figure out a safe zone today, or else no one will be there to pick her up from the ground.

My stop. I step off the bus, greeted by the familiar scent of sweat and gasoline, and take in the surroundings. The usual patches of green, or what passes for trees with their broken branches, look like failed attempts at nature. Our apartment buildings—those five-story Khrushchevs—are rundown, with entrances that reek of urine and walls painted despite the imposing code locks.

My ancestors were old-fashioned; they used to discipline me with a belt when I was a child, but I've grown up and become fierce. Now, my dad thinks twice before laying a hand on me. But as a child, I still remember the horror... and the lingering pain and discomfort afterward. My father enjoyed hitting me on my bare skin, as if I should admire the results, the jerk... I half expected him to try something when I turned fourteen. He didn't, and that's a relief.

I enter through the third entrance. Third entrance, third floor, flat fifty-one. The code lock is out of order, so I push the heavy door open, nearly slipping on someone's vomit. The stench of cat urine is overwhelming, even if you hold your breath, so I dash up to the third floor, unlock the two locks, and slip into the narrow hallway. Ah, much better.

"Hey everyone, I'm home!" I announce loudly before ducking into my room.

In my tiny room, there's a bed, a worn-out table that triggers an instinctual fear, a wardrobe overflowing with my belongings, and a drawer—reminders that I'm a girl, damn it all! That's where my bag belongs. Now, I have to change out of my pants and into a house dress, or they'll nag me endlessly. I can still recall the reasons from my childhood, but it's different now! I won't allow them to control me anymore; I'm stronger now, don't they understand that?

Fine, I'll do it anyway. As I slip into my jeans, I scan them for any traces of blood. It wasn't mine, of course, but I still need to be cautious; prison taught me that. I discard my T-shirt too, reluctantly donning the stupid dress.

Instantly, I feel vulnerable, stripped of my usual sense of security, which only serves to fuel my fury. Well, they brought it upon themselves; I didn't force their hand. Swathed in this soft blue attire of a reluctant girl, I make my way to the kitchen.

"Got a lot of F's?" Mom asks, wincing at my appearance. "If you don't study harder…"

"Are you going to use the sneakers you promised?" I retort sarcastically. "Or 'bring out the belt'? That ship has sailed, okay?"

"What a mouth you have," Mom sighs, placing her hand on her forehead wearily. "It's impossible to talk to you! If you hate it so much, maybe you should leave!"

"What? You're going to kick me out?" I hiss.

"You'll end up in an orphanage, you disgrace!" she shouts back.

And so begins our daily pointless and merciless argument, always ending in a stalemate. I retreat to my room, dismissing everyone with a sharp "fuck off," until Dad comes to mediate, as he calls it. It eventually quiets down, I'll give them that.

I should've waited, but I acted rashly. Who knew Mom would be watching me? It always worked before! I ran out of cigarettes, so I went to my ancestor's house to borrow fifty dollars for a pack, and there she was, with her wooden weapon. She screamed! I thought I was stronger for nothing. Now, I'm driving, nursing my arm, feeling clouded in the head from the altercation.

Someone at school will pay for this! I'll find a target to unleash my anger on, even if Mom is furious, despite the lack of physical punishment. But then, I'd end up in an orphanage for sure, which isn't in my interest. No matter, I'll find a way to get revenge; she'll regret ever raising her hand against me! She'll cry herself dry, and today, someone else will wipe away her tears.

My arm throbs with pain; I hope Mom didn't break it. She gripped my hair so tightly, I had to defend myself. Dad barely managed to pull her off, but now he's promised me a serious talk tonight. I'm sure he'll hit her; it's all he knows. Whatever, I'll find solace elsewhere; it won't be as terrifying. Mom scared me with her round stick and her wild eyes.

The bus pulls up in front of the school; I grab my bag with my uninjured hand and hop off the vehicle, only to spot Lerka stumbling away from me. Did I hit her so hard yesterday that she's still shaken? No, I didn't strike her hard enough to leave her faltering.

"Lerka, come here!" I call out to her, and she flinches, lowering her head before approaching.

"Hello, Masha," she stutters politely.

"Hi!" I reply casually, handing her my bag. "Follow me!"

She seems surprised; this gesture signifies not only forgiveness but also an assurance that she won't be targeted again. Yesterday was a one-time occurrence. She even appears cheerful, while I search for someone to unleash my anger on. I want to avenge the momentary fear that gripped me this morning, but the only people I encounter are fellow teenagers. And they scatter at the sight of Mad Mashka.

Oh! They're bringing in the new girl today; she'll be our new plaything. I won't strike her right away; who knows, maybe she's easygoing. Ha-ha. She'll undoubtedly become my favorite target, but not in my current mood.

I'm itching for a smoke, but I can't indulge just yet. If the teacher catches wind of it, she'll create a scene, that hysterical fool. Fine, I'll just be angrier. And with that mindset, I enter the classroom. Lerka hands me her bag with trembling hands. What did the girls do to her yesterday that she's shaking so much? Did Lariska overdo it? We'll have to discuss it during recess; Lerka is my toy.

The bell rings, signaling the start of English class. I find it tedious and unnecessary, like most subjects in this school. And the teacher, well, she's clueless, barely knowing ten words herself. The whole subject seems pointless, just like everything else here. I wonder if the next victim will be led to the slaughter or allowed a moment of respite before the inevitable. I can't wait to see who will grovel at my feet today, begging for mercy.

As the door creaks open, accompanied by the head teacher, my personal target for the day emerges. She appears fragile, dressed plainly, devoid of jewelry, her demeanor suggesting both vulnerability and defiance. No, she won't roar just yet; first, she'll endure the lessons, then she'll wish for a swift end. And the head teacher, she's smiling... Rumor has it she intimidates or even hits students in her office. But for now, I've managed to avoid her wrath.

"Meet the new girl," announces the head teacher. "Karina Strontseva will be joining your class. If Karina feels unwell, make sure to inform one of the teachers."

A snide comment from the boys prompts the head teacher's outrage. But there's an unspoken agreement among us: boys stick with boys, girls with girls, to avoid any scandals or conflicts during class. It's a pact we've made to keep the peace.

Meanwhile, I share a smirk with my roommate as we exchange a teasing glance that quickly spreads through the class. The game is on. As for the new girl, she attempts to sit next to Vaska Ipatov, who seems taken aback by her boldness. Even I wouldn't sit with him, especially wearing a skirt. Looks like it's going to be an eventful day...

As the lesson begins, I observe Vaska's actions. The new girl flinches, clearly uncomfortable, and I grin knowingly.

Ipatov has a reputation for crossing boundaries, which is why you only confront him with a fist. It appears he's probing the new girl with his usual sneer, but her response leaves him visibly shaken. I don't understand...

Later, after class, Ipatov approaches me. "Mashka, don't mess with Karinka," he pleads. "Her mother passed away a week ago. It wouldn't be right."

"Her ancestors powerful or something?" I jest.

"No, she's an orphan," Vaska explains sadly. "It's just not right, you know?"

"And you've suddenly developed a conscience for an orphan," I sneer, delivering a sharp kick to his groin.

"Madness, what are you doing?!" protests Petyka, our lookout.

In a few words, I explain the situation to him, leaving him red-faced. Vaska will pay for his transgression tonight, as per our agreement. But the fact that Karina is an orphan, with no one to defend her, is good news to me.

Karina seems to sense something... While I deal with Vaska, she slips away unnoticed. But it's only a matter of time before she faces my wrath, and I'll be even angrier tomorrow, based on what I've endured today. But for now, I have Petyka and Vaska to deal with—they've been asking for it for a long time ...

EVIL BEGETS EVIL

ELDER

IN VAIN, I believed myself stronger than my ancestors. Now, all I can think about is the pain. They twisted me just like they did when I was a child, and then my father lashed out, relentlessly, until I bled. I cried out like a child, but it made no difference. Now, I lie in bed, tears streaming down my face, consumed by agony. My entire body aches—my back, legs, and especially my buttocks, throbbing with pain. It's almost unbearable, pushing me to the brink of unconsciousness.

The pain is excruciating, making even the slightest movement unbearable. I can't help but cry into my pillow. The question of "why" seems futile; the reason is clear. If my mother hadn't burned my father's wallet, none of this would have happened. But now... they've lost their minds, promising more punishment tomorrow. Somehow, I believe them—they'll beat me every day until I put an end to them in my sleep. And I will, as soon as I can walk again.

She wet herself while they beat her, like a frightened kitten. I'll surely end them both for this, consequences be damned! I'll make them suffer... But my fury quickly gives way to fear. The thought of my father violating me, just to "teach" me a lesson, sends shivers down my spine. I tremble at the mere idea.

Gathering my resolve, I listen for any sounds outside the door. It's quiet, so I force myself to get up, if only to wash off the blood. I can't even put my pants on due to the pain. Where are they now? I dread what awaits me next, even though they've promised to leave me alone. Perhaps it's just another tactic to frighten me. I can't endure it a second time. Maybe I should stab them before it's too late.

With caution, I step out of the room and hurry to the bathroom, locking the door behind me. I feel like I'm losing my mind... I need to channel my anger. I need to be furious and take control before they destroy me. My mother seems to enjoy the spectacle, and the feeling of helplessness still haunts me.

From the sounds of it, they revel in their cruelty... I'm certain they relished beating me, and now they're not done yet. What should I do? I must come up with a plan; I refuse to be a pawn in their twisted games. If the girls find my traces in the bathroom, I'll lose my authority. I'll be subjected to endless torment...

With these thoughts racing through my mind, I hastily clean myself up and return to my room, barricading the door with a chair. Glancing at my bruised buttocks in the bathroom mirror, I wonder how I'll even walk or sit tomorrow.

I've been trying to sleep, but the pain won't let me. And then there's the fear, lurking in the depths of my mind. Across the street, the windows of the nine-story building glow dimly. People live there too, perhaps just as monstrous as my ancestors... My thoughts drift to the new girl. Tomorrow, half the school will know the rumors about her, and then she'll face my wrath. She'll beg for mercy, and tonight, I'll arm myself with a knife and prepare for their onslaught. I hate them all!

As if the day weren't enough, the night brings nightmares. I'm bound to a board, helpless as my tormentors approach. I'd rather endure the beatings than suffer these dreams. Each time, I wake up screaming, unable to escape the terror.

In the morning, sleep-deprived and seething with anger, I avoid my parents and grab a bun for breakfast. I ignore my mother's muttering and rush out of the house, eager to escape their grasp. Walking is painful, my tight jeans exacerbating the discomfort with every step. It makes me want to lash out, to make someone else feel my pain. And I know who will bear the brunt of my rage tonight!

Exiting the bus, I scan the bus stop for Lerka, but she's nowhere to be seen. How dare she not greet me? I'll show her! Bursting into the school, I search for her, fueled by fury. But Lerka is absent. Where could she have gone?

The bell rings, interrupting my search. Lerka's absence is announced by the class teacher, who speaks softly. Last night, Lerka suffered a heart attack and passed away. It doesn't affect me; it only annoys me—I need to find a new target. But one of the girls is sobbing. I can't comprehend who would be so pathetic. Tanya?! Unexpectedly, even the cold, angry Tanya is emotional. The class teacher reassures us, reminding us that anyone's heart could fail at any moment.

The new girl sits next to Vaska, whispering to him. It seems he's warning her about who to fear, but it won't save her. Gym class is the final lesson, where anything can happen... Maybe I'll skip class, but I'll still get her! I need to release my pent-up anger before I explode

Vaska's sudden interest in the new girl has become apparent. He practically escorted her to the restroom, where she ended up with gum tangled in her hair after he prevented her from pulling up her skirt, giving her a swift smack that sent her sprawling to the floor. The others laughed, making crude jokes about "Karina's adventures with the penguin," as my father might say. Despite the humiliation, she doesn't react, and it's clear that Vaska wants to claim her as his own.

When a boy claims a girl, she becomes off-limits to others, but he bears the responsibility for her, so not many are willing to take that risk. However, Vaska has a history of troublemaking, so it's entirely possible, which means we need to intervene before he does. It won't happen today, as it doesn't align with the boys' plans, so most likely, it will happen tomorrow. But I'll make sure she's begging at my feet by then—or I'm not Mad Mashka!

In class, the new girl sits with Vaska, making it impossible for me to approach her. During recess, the girls taunt her, but she remains unfazed, which infuriates me to no end. I clench my fists, feeling a surge of anger as I navigate the restroom alone, ensuring that no one sees the bruises on my behind. It stings to urinate, just like yesterday. Damn my ancestors for their cruelty—I could strangle them!

The teachers, sensing my agitation, don't inquire further, and with each passing lesson, my anger intensifies. The girls notice, keeping their distance, but gym class looms ahead, forcing me to maintain my composure. Vaska won't be in our changing room, and she'll start changing there, setting the stage for...

I opt for sports pants instead of the usual gym shorts, defying the gym teacher's expectations. Though he knows me well—recall the incident from a year ago when I kicked him in the groin—he doesn't say a word. As we commence the class, the new girl, seemingly unaffected by the previous incidents, joins in the activities. However, she soon falls, courtesy of the other girls' mischief. Though unscathed, it's evident she's out of her depth—a sight that brings a smirk to my face.

Suddenly, I feel a sharp pain as a ball strikes my rear end. It's excruciating, and I turn to see Vaska grinning maliciously. Enraged, I launch myself at him, pummeling him with all my might. He tries to fight back, but I'm fueled by rage, striking him relentlessly.

My fellow classmates intervene, dousing me with water to calm me down. Slowly regaining my senses, I see Vaska being escorted away, unconscious. Did I kill him?

"He's alive," one of the boys reassures me. "You really went crazy, Mad..."

Karina looks at me with horror, but as they take Vaska to the medical center—without calling an ambulance, as it's Evseich's fault, and they all cover for each other—I feel a surge of satisfaction. Karina is left defenseless, a fact that fills me with glee. She doesn't realize it, foolishly believing that since nothing happened before class, I'll spare her afterward. She's a fool.

As we head to the changing room, I quickly exchange nods with the girls, giving them instructions. This is going to be fun. Perhaps I'll make her prance around naked. But first, the entertainment!

She begins to change, and when she's down to her underwear, Lariska and Tanka pounce on her. Karina tries to scream, but they quickly stuff her gym shorts into her mouth, stripping her completely. I take the wire in hand, watching gleefully as the welts rise with each strike. But I tire too quickly, as if my fuse has been extinguished.

"On your knees, worm!" I order once she's released. She lies there, whimpering, and I continue to strike her, commanding her to kneel. She tries to stand, but I seize her by the chain around her neck, forcing her into submission. But we're not done yet.

As I pull on the chain, it snaps, and I reel back in anger. Before I can react, Karina lunges at me, striking me with unexpected force. I stagger backward, trying to fend her off, but I lose my balance and fall.

Something crunches beneath me, and suddenly, I'm overwhelmed by searing pain. It's unbearable, consuming me entirely. Panic sets in as I realize I can't move. The agony intensifies, and the world around me fades to darkness.

In the void, a voice speaks. "You will be punished for the evil you have done."

"Who are you?" I try to ask, but there's no response—only the relentless agony.

Is this what they wanted—to switch me off and end my life?

ORPHAN

ELDER

I OPEN MY EYES. The first thing I notice is that there is no discomfort, and I can breathe without those terrible tubes. That appears to be the end of the news—at least the positive news. My arms are weak and barely moving, as are my legs. It's as if they don't exist and I can't reach out to feel them. Did they cut them off? No, it cannot be; why should it be?

I'm certainly in the hospital, but I'm not sure what's going on. But I believe they will tell me sooner or later. I heard my mother's angry, cruel final words, but I believe they were a continuation of the dream; I can't expect my mother to want me dead, can she? I inhale and exhale, attempting to figure out what is going on. My mouth is dry as a desert, my mind is buzzing, and I'm feeling a little ill. And the sensation of complete helplessness is more terrible than ever.

The door opens, someone enters... A woman in green, maybe a doctor, maybe a nurse. More likely a nurse, judging by the grumbling. I struggle to part my lips to ask something, but at that moment she sees me lying there with my eyes open.

"Drink..." I wheeze, pushing the word through parched lips.

"You're awake now," the woman murmured softly. Shortly after, she gently nudged my lips and encouraged, "Take a drink, the doctor will be here shortly."

I sip on the unexpectedly delicious water and realize that I likely haven't had a drink in about a month. I feel a surge of questions brewing within me, but the nurse swiftly takes the drink away from me and departs. I make a mental note to inform my father of their rudeness later. However, the act of drinking does clear my mind slightly, so I attempt to distinguish between what was a dream and what was reality, but I am unsuccessful. As I ponder this, the door opens once more, and a man dressed in green enters, accompanied by someone else whom I cannot discern.

The doctor, likely, announced cheerfully, "Masha is awake now. She was in a coma for a week, but she's come around."

"Those girls who were brought in from school?" Someone asks from behind him.

"They are," he nods. The nature of the skin damage is the same, which is why this case is interesting.

"Well, this one's got it all figured out," said another voice, a male voice, I think.

"We'll see about that in a moment," the doctor informs her and simply tosses the blanket aside.

I realize I'm lying naked and want to cover myself, but my hands are barely moving, so I do so slowly. With a forceful gesture, my hands move away from me, and then do something to shield my body from me. I can't tell what they're doing; I don't feel anything at all; it feels like they're just thinking. But then they start sticking my hands with needles, causing me to cry out.

"So, despite the surgical intervention, we have partial paralysis, - concludes the doctor. - The legs are completely paralysed, there are no reflexes, the thighs are partially touched, there is no sensitivity of the genitals.

"It could have been worse," some woman shrugged indifferently. - At least my hands are working, so I'm lucky.

"Yeah, I guess so," nods the man, "at least he'll be able to move.

What is this? Am I a cripple now? This can't be happening! It can't happen to me! But I guess mine can beat me all they want, I'm completely at their mercy. It's Carina! The new snot, I'll get her! I'll strangle her, that bitch! I can't be a cripple, not again!

I seem to shout something, demand something, but I am simply ignored. After a while, the nurse from earlier enters the room again, looking at me with squeamishness. She sighs heavily and pulls back the blanket, exposing me completely again. I attempt to pull the blanket over myself, but instantly receive a sharp slap on the wrist.

She complained that there were many disabled people and suggested that they should euthanize them or dispose of them like unwanted objects. Then, she wiped me with something cold, remarking that I was just lying there, occupying space.

"Damn you!" I shout, shrieking. "I'm going to tell Dad!"

"You don't have a daddy," she informs me. And you don't have a mum. You're an orphan and a cripple, so you're going to lie still and stay out of my way, okay?

For some reason, I immediately believed her. I know she was telling the truth, and the ancestors, it turns out, gave up on me. But why? Why? So Mum's comments were true? I should've murdered them! I should've murdered them! I'll get out of here, I'll cut all of them, and they'll blow bloody bubbles, traitors, I'll kill them all... all of them!

What will happen to me? That is the question. If mine kicked me out, what now? Orphanage? Or what? I have no notion what I'll do. This news makes me want to scream, hurt someone, and flee. But I can't get away because my arms and legs won't support me. I do not have legs anymore. But I do not want to! I do not want to! I would rather murder you! You bastards!

"Kill me, you bastards!" I shout loudly. "You bastards, you bastards, kill me!"

The door swings open abruptly, and the nurse from

earlier enters the room and slaps my cheeks hard, once, again, again, again, again! My head whips around, my scream is interrupted, and I stare at her dumbfounded, ready to cry, but somehow an imposing fist appears in front of my nose, which makes it clear to me that screaming is not allowed here, so I cry, quietly crying, trying to hold back, to suppress my sobs.

I begin to realise that I am all alone. Nobody comes to see me except the doctor and the nurses. They do not treat me with ceremony - they wash me, climb everywhere, and very harshly suppress my hysterics. In doing so, it suddenly appears that my arse has at least partially retained sensitivity. The good news is that at least I won't shit under myself, but the bad news is... I can feel all the injections perfectly. And they hurt like hell, and I feel like they're taking revenge on me.

Nothing, even from the pram, can stop me from strangling them; just let me out, and you will all be sorry! All of you! I'll get out and slay all of you drowsy ones! I'll start with the nurses, then the disloyal ancestors, and finally Carina. I'll kill her gradually, so she'll take a long time to die, you rat! I couldn't murder her in the same way a human would!

But the door opens again, and the thing in the green uniform hurts me so badly that I wriggle and scream, and she slaps me on the fresh injection with the palm of her hand so hard that I almost faint from the pain. As if someone paid them... Or maybe they did? The same Vaska - his ancestors have a lot of money, can he take revenge like that? It's easy! He's as bad as that bitch...

I'm helpless in the hospital. They can do anything to me, and I won't be able to say a word. Except for the sadistic nurse, nobody cares about me. Not a soul. At least she's paying attention, though. After a week or two, I'll take any attention I can get, even if it means getting hurt. I can't stand being alone.

Suddenly, I realize it's all my fault. I'm a very bad girl, so everything is deserved. It's okay that they hurt me, it's okay that I'm alone. I don't want to live, but I have to. Today, I was moved into a room that will now be my home forever. I have nothing and no one. No home, no parents... Today, a woman is coming from that... that orphanage deal.

I wonder if I'll get anything for school. The gym teacher will go to jail, it seems, and me... The girls didn't say anything, and the new girl isn't talking. They say she had a severe emotional shock, and now she's in a bad way. And it's my fault. I'm guilty of everything. I even tried to tell it to the investigator, but he just sadly smiled and left. He didn't believe me. Only the evil nurses believe that I am bad. They never deny themselves the opportunity to hurt me.

They don't talk to me; they just ignore any attempts to talk to them. If I shout, they just smack me on the mouth, and that's it. It's like I'm some kind of outcast. I think I'm going crazy, but somehow I'm not. The traitor parents don't even show up; they just abandoned me, and that's it. I'm going to kill them anyway! Even if it's not right now, I'll kill them! Damn things...

It's my own fault, but they're parents; they have to! I don't want to be like this! I don't want to be like this! Ouch! Why?

"For what?!" I jump up.

"You're the one who tortured Karinka, you bitch..." I heard a reply for the first time in a long time. Not even an answer, just a hiss. "You, no matter what they say, I know! For Strontseva, you are not enough to kill, but you will live. Live and remember!"

And then I realize they're really after me. But who are they? Why are they now... Although I understand why... After all, I really, it turns out, tortured the new girl. And got my payback, apparently, overflowing someone's cup of patience. So I put my head down and shut up, because they're right. And I deserve it.

After that, I do a lot of thinking. They leave me alone, without locking the window or hiding any stabbing things. They probably hope I'll kill myself, but I just can't. I even took a knife in my hand once; it would have seemed easy, but I just couldn't. So I lie there and remember all the people I beat and abused. They begged for mercy and then cursed me, but I didn't believe that those curses were worth anything.

Now I had to believe it, because I guess they had caught up with me.

"Here?" I hear a calm and somewhat indifferent voice, snapping me out of my thoughts. "Another cripple?"

"Yes, but her hands are working and she can look after herself," my doctor's voice answers her. "Please."

A burly lady in a suit enters the room with a squeamish look. It is understandable; she came to see an invalid, although everyone here with some sadistic pleasure calls me a cripple, as if they like my tears. But maybe they do, who knows... So this lady comes in, takes a chair, and sits down next to my bed.

"So, you're Maria Nefedova," she told me with an unfamiliar surname. "Your foster parents disinherited you, so you can't have their surname."

Another devastating blow - I wasn't family, so they didn't owe me anything. That's only for relatives, and I, it turns out... That's why they threw me out. Why do they need me like that, everything is right, there's nothing to take revenge for. The woman from the guardianship office makes sure that the information has reached me and continues.

"Even though you seem to be able to get care, you will go to a hospice first," she tells me. "There is no room for you in the orphanage, but at least you will have someone to look after you."

"And... When?" I ask quietly, remembering what "hospice" means.

"The day after tomorrow," she said, smiling at me. "You'll be discharged, and the hospice will take care of your rehabilitation. There's no need..."

I realize what she means - there's no point in taking up space, because I'm nobody. I'm fourteen years old and my life is over. I have no life at all, because I'm almost helpless and nobody wants me. They won't even hire me in a brothel with my sensitivity. So my destiny... What is my destiny? I don't know, I just want to be gone. If I had a chance to start over, or at least heal my legs, I would! I'd give it to all of them! I'd...

She leaves, and I cry quietly into my pillow. Soon the nurses will come and give me very painful, though unnecessary injections. Unnecessary because I am being discharged, and painful because they like it that way, and they can't hit me - they will be punished for marks. All I can do is resign myself to it and hope that one day I can start again. Maybe I could climb out the window.

No, it's a very bad idea, because if they save me, they'll send me to a mental institution forever, and a mental institution is worse than any orphanage - there's no way out. Even theoretically there is no way out, which makes me want to cry bitterly, because I can't live like that, but I don't want to go to the asylum.

Why am I suddenly changing so much, it seems like just yesterday I hated everyone and now I just don't care? I think it's the not talking to me and getting revenge. I just seem to be losing the will to live. Maybe I should try contacting some of the girls. What's the point? Just to make them laugh? Fuck them all! Fuck them all, fuck them all! I hate bastards!

If it wasn't for this school, if it wasn't for these foster parents, maybe I wouldn't be so mean! It's all their fault, they made me like this, they made me be a beast! I'm a beast and a very bad girl, and I've paid for that and more than once... But it's not my fault, because it's them! They made me this way! They're the ones who should be beaten! They're the ones who should be hurt! They're the ones who should get revenge, not me!

I was a kid and I got beaten up at home, beaten up at school, what did they expect? A pink baby at the end? So I got mad! Yes! It's all them.

I'm not just crying, I'm howling because nothing can be changed, I'm howling, huddled together because I'm about to be beaten, but I'm roaring at the top of my voice. Somebody avenge me!

HOSPICE

ELDER

The nurses accompany me out of the hospital, and I feel like I want to die. I wish I could do it myself, but I'm not given the chance. They guide me downstairs and seat me in an ambulance, which lacks doctors or sirens. It's just a transport vehicle, the driver informs me, so there's no rush.

"If you decide to die," he tells me, "I'll just take you to the morgue."

"Why?" I ask him quietly, but he either doesn't hear me or ignores me.

The car suddenly starts, making me feel nauseous almost instantly, but I hold onto the seat, feeling like I'm spinning like a blender. I don't understand why even strangers treat me this way - as if I'm a pariah, or as if I have "kick her - very bad girl" written all over me. It can't be that everyone wants revenge on me! Or... could it? Is this my fate from now on?

I imagine myself being alone forever, surrounded by indifference, angry words, and hatred, feeling like I'm about to faint. I try to keep it together, but somehow I can't, and everything fades away. But then I feel a hard blow to my face, jolting my eyelids open in surprise. The car has stopped, and above me, I see a stout woman in a dirty white gown, looking at me with an odd expression.

"So, are we taking her to the morgue?" comes a cheerful voice from somewhere, which I recognize as the driver's a moment later.

"She'll survive yet," the woman chuckles, then turns and orders, "Take her to the fourth floor; they'll sort out where to put her."

Somebody must have paid them off! Someone paid them all to hate me, because it can't be like this! People can't be like this... They just can't! These thoughts make me start to cry, but no one seems to care. It seems like nobody cares about me at all, and when the driver places me in the wheelchair, he squeezes my breasts so hard it hurts, making me scream.

Then suddenly I find myself inside very quickly. My head is spinning, my heart is racing, and I'm crying because the driver hurt me so much. But he hands me over to some woman, and I... I brace myself for the pain, but I don't expect what happens next.

"And here we have Mashenka," some woman smiles

falsely. "They paid well for Mashenka," she adds. "So she'll have special conditions."

I knew it! I knew they weren't just bastards; they were in it for the money! What's going to happen to me now? What? The woman guides me down the corridor, showing me rooms where children are dying, but their parents are by their side. Stroking, playing, speaking lovingly... This woman shows me, quietly commenting:

"And here we have Tanechka," she informs me with a smile. "She doesn't have more than a week to live, but her parents love her anyway, see?"

"Don't..." I ask her, realizing pleading is futile.

"You have to, you little bastard, you have to," my escort says with the same affectionate smile. "You will have a lot of pain ahead of you, just like her, but there is no one to love you."

"No... No... No... No..." I whisper, realizing I'm condemned.

I'll never escape from here; they'll drive me crazy. They must have been paid to do that, so there's no way out, and they won't let me die before my time. Then they'll poison me with some slow toxin to prolong my suffering. If Vaska paid for it, then that's exactly what's going to happen.

They take me around and show me children who have no future but have parents who love them. I remember myself and my childhood, realizing that I have never had such a thing and will never have it, which fills my heart with pain.

Just the pain of realization... Because now I see what has always been kept from me by a cloudy glass.

I'm a very bad girl, and I realize it now, but in my opinion, torturing like this is not punishment, it is torture. Like the Nazis...

But then the wheelchair reaches the last room, and they take me there. There is a strange thing here - the other rooms are single rooms, and there is someone here. I can't see who it is because tears blur my vision. I can't stop crying, so I can't see much in front of me. And the woman, whose cigarette smoke makes me feel nauseous, not very politely moves me onto the bed.

"This is where you're going to live," she says, her voice full of satisfaction. "Right next to your best friend. It'll be less boring for both of you."

Best friend? But I don't have any, and it's unlikely any of the girls would even get in here, so it's more of a taunt. Who would they call that? I don't even have an idea. After informing me of the feeding time, the woman leaves, and I bury my face in my pillow to cry. There is not a single thought in my head, only one question - why? Why is this happening to me? I am... I am... and then Lerka, Tanya, that girl... they pass in front of my eyes, and Karina closes the row. Pictures of humiliation, blood, beaten girls begging for something, screwed into my brain, more and more painful, making me almost lose touch with reality.

It hurts, it really hurts; I want to erase that memory...

Lerka howling under the belt... Tanya on her knees, naked, urinating... Larka smearing blood on her face... And... And... And... And... And... Was it all me? Did I do it? Me? No! And then the lights go out.

I open my eyes, wanting to look at my neighbor, and immediately regret it. On the bed, staring at the ceiling, lying immovably... Karina. No! Don't! Kill her! Don't! When I see her, I scream, screaming as hard as I can, wishing someone would come, to shield her from me, to do something! But no one comes, it's like there's no one left in the whole hospice, and I'm screaming my throat out.

My scream echoes in the room, where there is no one but me and an unresponsive Karina. She just stares at the ceiling and that's it, not reacting to anything. For a moment, I think she's dead, but she's not; I even wish she was, but I can't do anything on my own right now - my arms are too weak. The only thing I can do is scream...

They want to drive me crazy, I can see it very well, but I can't do anything about it because now I am completely helpless, as if condemned to a slow death. I even begin to think that someone is watching me through the peephole in the door and smiling happily at my torment.

"You're probably wondering why they did this to you," I hear a familiar voice.

Vaska enters the room. I've just been bathed, so I'm wearing nothing under the blanket - they'll put a diaper on me later - and Vaska seems to know it. Maybe they washed me just for him... He comes up to Karina, strokes her head, and then turns to me, looking at me in a way that makes me afraid.

"As long as you were adopted, my father wasn't interested in you," Vaska explained to me. "Do you understand, sister?" he says with a sneer.

"Sis?" I wonder, realizing now why he was so interested in paying for me.

"You're your father's illegitimate child," the guy continues, yanking the blanket up sharply, exposing me completely naked to him. "What a hottie!" he admires. "Your guardians broke the contract, and they're sorry. In concrete. But you..."

I'll be killed. I realize it very well - his father does not need extra heiresses, and I can be used.... Vaska approaches me and bends my legs skillfully so that my most private part is exposed. I realize what he sees, and I reach out to cover myself with my hands, but he slaps me across the face.

"My father doesn't care how you die," Vaska says. "That's why he just gave you the money, so you wouldn't occupy space. Do you think anyone will save you?"

I know there's no escape, and I realize what's about to happen, but I have no sensitivity down there, so he's unlikely to be interested himself. But then I remember how guys reacted to jokes about privates, and I smile through my tears. Vaska is clearly furious, frantically unbuttoning his trousers.

"That's it?" I say, as mockingly as I can. "Did you borrow a dwarf's thing?"

"You bastard!" A furious Vaska punches me in the face, then something crunches in my chest under his fist, then... I don't remember.

When I open my eyes again, Vaska is gone. My whole body hurts, and it still hurts to breathe. Whether he did something to me or not, I don't know, and I don't really care. I realize now why I'm being treated this way. It's not about Karina not showing signs of life. It's that I can claim my inheritance, that's all. So I'm going to die here, and my last days will be very painful.

These thoughts bring back memories. For as long as I can remember, I wasn't exactly a favorite child. It could come at any time, so I quickly learned to hide. And then, as I grew older, I learned to fight back, even though I realize I wasn't fighting with my full strength. The fact that I even got custody for money doesn't surprise me at all. How can anything surprise you these days?

I had to fight my way through school, but when I became just a cruel person, I don't understand. Karina could have been left alone, and there was no reason to beat up Lerka like that. I must be really rabid, so I'm right. After all, rabid animals are killed, and now I will be killed. First, they'll beat me long and often to make me crazy, and then they'll put me to sleep... or drown me... I wonder how they'll kill me? Is it some kind of elaborate method, or just an injection of some kind? I remember reading somewhere that it can be done quite easily if the patient is immovable...

The door opens, and a fat, angry woman enters the room with a tray. Now there will be lunch... Some kind of mush instead of soup, porridge, bread, tea... I am already getting used to such food and to waiting for death, talking to Karina in between, even though I know she can't hear me. I already know everything... I am not heard, not understood, and I am doomed, because there is no way out.

I think I am dying, because time is merging into a single streak, gray like my life, and the only book here is the Bible. That's what I'm reading, just so I don't have to think about anything. But I can't think about anything at all. At least the nurses don't forget about me, bringing me pain every day. And that pain shows that I'm alive. There seems to be no way out, no way in, so I just resign myself to waiting for death.

Death, however, does not come to me. My neighbor, whose name I no longer remember, dies in the night. I don't remember my name either, it seems, because I am called a "corpse" and a "creature". They leave her dead, not trying to get her out quickly, but then something happens that makes everyone start running around, so much so that they even forget to bring me the pain with my breakfast. I don't know what that has to do with...

The answer arrives in the afternoon with a distinguished-looking man in his forties, I guess. When I see him, I sigh. A man can come to me for one purpose, I think, so I pull down the thin blanket with my hands to hide my face in it. I think Vaska hurt my ribs when he hit me, because I haven't been breathing very well since, but that's all the same, I think. So, he looks at me carefully, and to what I'm ready for, sighs, silently turns on his side and starts yelling.

In an hour, I'm leaving the hospice, which is full of rubbish. But I don't care, because I don't expect anything good in life. In an hour, I'll be leaving the hospice, a place filled with sadness and despair. But honestly, I'm past caring because I've lost hope for anything good in life. Maybe time will prove me right or wrong, but right now, I don't even have the strength to speak. My energy is depleted; all I can do is gaze out the window.

This time, the driver is unexpectedly kind and attentive. He gently pats my head, helps me into the seat, and secures my seatbelt. I'm taken aback by his compassion. As we drive off, he seems to handle me with care, though I'm puzzled as to why.

I don't really care where we're headed, to be honest. It doesn't matter much to me because I feel like I'm nearing the end of my life. Sooner or later, I'll meet my fate, whether it's at the hands of Vaska's father or through some other means. And then, I'll probably regret many things for a long time, until... until whatever is meant to happen, happens.

I've been dealt a rough hand my whole life, and now I'm

just weary. I'm tired of feeling worthless, helpless, and abandoned. To be honest, I'm even starting to lose my grip on reality... It feels like ages pass as we travel, and I can't even comprehend why or where I'm going.

Outside, snowflakes drift past the window, carrying some hidden significance that escapes me. I've forgotten so much - my name, my age, even who I am. All I know is that I'm a girl, different from a boy, but I don't understand why or what purpose it serves. My memory is fading, but I still recall being labeled a "bad girl." Perhaps someone thought they could change me for the better, but it seems they went too far. And I can't shake the memory of Vasya, the boy who once beat me... Was he trying to teach me a lesson?

THE GHOST OF SALVATION

ELDER

I WAKE up to the sight of dull grey walls in the hospice. It feels like I just had a dream where I was taken away somewhere and forgot everything. There's no easy way out, no salvation; I don't deserve it. None of it. So, I resign myself to awaiting my death because my life is over. I wonder if Karina is still alive, but what kind of life would that be?

The door creaks open, and I spot my tormentor holding a syringe. I shut my eyes, bracing myself for the pain. These injections, I don't know what they are, but they don't ease my suffering. Every day, the agony continues, but I've grown accustomed to it. It's become routine - pain in the morning, humiliation at night, no matter the form.

"Are you dead?" my tormentor muses before abruptly leaving, leaving me to dwell on Karina's likely demise, just like in my dream. She was fortunate, but for me, the wait goes on. Soon, they'll take her away, and my day will proceed as usual - silent, painful, and devoid of attention. That's all I seem to deserve.

Then, a surprised man's voice breaks the silence, but I keep my eyes shut. If he's a man, he's likely here for one thing only. I don't want to see him. I hear frantic murmurs between my tormentor and the newcomer before I'm turned around. This will hurt, I know it. I quietly sob, expecting the worst, but then I'm gently returned to my previous position.

"What kind of place is this?" the man's voice rings with authority. "Why is she here?"

His words surprise and terrify me even more. I don't understand what's happening, but there's a flurry of activity around me. I'm cautiously lifted onto a stretcher, and they crudely remark about my appearance and nudity. I'm too afraid to open my eyes, fearing Vaska's father's impatience and my impending demise. Perhaps they'll take me to the woods, dig a grave, and bury me alive. The thought alone makes me tremble.

"Oh God, what's wrong with her?" a woman's voice exclaims. "She's trembling!"

"She's probably terrified," the man replies. "Look at her, she's like a child from a concentration camp. Malnourished, neglected, injected with magnesia... her heart must be in terrible shape."

"Let's go!" the woman commands, and suddenly, a siren blares above me.

It seems we're in an ambulance, but why? Why have they decided to save me? Or is this just a ploy before my demise? Fear grips me as warm arms envelop me, and I can't help but cry bitterly. I shake uncontrollably and weep, yet no one reprimands me. Maybe it's okay to feel human one last time...

"Are we... being buried?" I manage to choke out.

"Hush, dear," a kind, unfamiliar woman soothes me. "The worst is over; no one's going to bury you."

"What's going on?" someone asks.

"She thinks we're taking her to bury her," the woman sighs.

Then, I realize it's all a dream. It can't be real because... because it's me, and good things don't happen to me. Yet, in this extraordinary dream, I'm being rescued. I know deep down there's no one coming to save me, for what reason? But hope flickers to life. Here, I can cry freely, feel human, escape my reality... If only I could stay here forever!

The car halts, and the stretcher carrying me rushes somewhere. My ears buzz, and I catch fragments of words: exhaustion, torture, concentration camp. I don't understand how they relate to me; I've just been condemned. But then, they start probing me... touching me... I keep my eyes shut, fearing the dream will vanish, replaced by the usual nightmare.

"Why are your eyes closed?" someone inquires.

"The child's scared," a woman's voice replies. "She's too frightened; don't rush her. The transition is too abrupt for her."

"Rib fractures, abscess, lesions..." someone dictates hurriedly. A prick on my arm, and everything fades away.

Dead Karina stares at me. So does dead Lerka, both silent witnesses as I lie in a pit. Karina tosses a handful of earth at me, followed by Lerka. They bury me alive, and I'm paralyzed. Earth piles up faster than they throw it, as if everyone I've wronged is now burying me, erasing me from their lives forever. Monsters! They'll kill me! They'll kill me unjustly! What do they care!

I scream and scream, but the earth keeps coming, suffocating me slowly. I want to scream in despair, curse them all, but I can't, it feels like I can't do anything...

Then, as the earth fills my mouth, suffocating me, a strong wind gusts. It blows away the earth, making me gasp for air. I don't know who or what is helping me, but I'm grateful! The wind sweeps away Karina and Lerka, clearing the earth around me, and the sky above turns blue. I don't know what it means, but I smile because I feel free. And then, something happens...

"You're awake, thank goodness," an unfamiliar man's voice says. "Breathe, little one, breathe..."

They transfer me from the hospital to a place called a sanatorium, a small house where some grandparents live, almost in the woods. The uncle who brings me here says I should stay for a while. But I don't really care because it feels like I've been stuck in the same pit I dreamt about under anesthesia. It's like I don't exist, like the grandmothers can see me but don't want to talk to me, leaving me alone again.

At the hospital, a doctor hugged me, but only after the anesthesia did I feel like a little girl. I call everyone uncle and auntie here, and they're kind to me. It feels amazing, hard to describe. I feel accepted and not ugly or repulsive, at least that's how it feels. There's no beating here, and the aunt who brings me food is gentle. She even hugs me sometimes, though it's rare, and I don't feel worthy of it.

Now, at the sanatorium, I'm back in my wheelchair. I can move around a bit, especially since I enjoy being outside and breathing fresh air, even though I still remember the dirt falling on my face. Somehow, being outdoors doesn't make me feel as isolated. It's fascinating; there are so many different sounds to listen to.

Maybe Mashka really stayed in that pit, and now only a shell remains. Every day, I realize more and more how bad I was. Maybe that's why I was rightly punished in the hospice, left all alone because nobody wants me. I did everything wrong - I hurt the girls and the boys, scolded my mom and dad, so I deserved the punishment. Maybe God looked at me, a nasty girl, and decided I needed punishment to become good. But I didn't become good, so they punished me even more.

I remember everything I did, but now it feels like it wasn't me, but an evil version of myself, like the one the girls buried alive. I know that evil version is still me, but I don't want to be like that. I want to be a little baby so I can hide, away from everyone. Because I'm scared, so scared I can't even explain it.

The grandmothers look at me as if I'm about to steal something from them, as if they'll beat me. That makes it even scarier. Maybe they know I've been very bad and want to punish me, but they're not allowed to, or they're not interested. I don't feel much of anything anymore. Maybe to want to punish someone, you have to feel it. Maybe adults need their kids to cry and scream in pain. But why?

Okay, I'm bad, so maybe I need to scream and cry to feel better, but what about others? Do only bad people like me get punished? I should ask, but I'm afraid of the grandmothers; they have long, thick sticks, and what if they beat me? Then they'll break me, and they'll be sorry they did.

I don't know who to ask, but there's already a lot of snow outside, and we have a Christmas tree by our front door. I like being near it; it makes me feel like a little girl again, like miracles are possible. But maybe not, because when everyone goes out to celebrate, I'm never invited. I feel so lonely, almost to the point of tears. So I put on my fur coat and roll into the woods, imagining I'm the last person alive. I like to think that all the people suddenly disappeared, and I'm alone. So, I roll outside where it's freezing, only the stars shining.

I roll a little, but it's hard to turn the wheels; my arms get tired quickly. Then, a shadow appears, and the stroller starts moving faster and faster into the forest. I open my mouth to scream when something hits me hard in the face, so hard I taste blood and my eyes blur like tears. Suddenly, the stroller flips over, and I fall face-first into the snow.

"When are you going to die?" someone hisses, ripping off my coat, leaving me shivering. I try to get up, but there's nothing but woods around me, and it's freezing. Then I realize Vaska's dad brought me here too, so I'm going to die. I can't see my wheelchair, my hands are numb, so I lie down in the snow, deciding to wait until I freeze. They say it doesn't hurt; you just fall asleep, and that's it.

"Who's that?" a deep voice interrupts.

Suddenly, I'm lifted into the air and see an uncle in a red coat adorned with shining stones and patterns. Beside him stands a girl about twelve years old, wearing a blue coat. The uncle frowns at me, sending shivers down my spine.

"What's wrong with her, Grandpa?" the girl asks, intrigued.

"This girl was very bad; she almost killed two people," Grandpa explains. "She got punished for it, but she's being tortured, so she doesn't realize it."

"Oh..." the girl in blue gasps. "So she's in pain but doesn't know it? Oh... What now?"

"Now it's a choice!" Ded Moroz* declares. "What do you want, child - legs or a family?"

If I'm dying anyway, does it matter? Especially since I don't feel cold anymore. But if it were real, what would I choose? My legs? Vaska's dad will find me and kill me; I can't run away from him. And who knows what they'll do to me alone. And if they beat me... I'm defenseless! No, I'm scared, so scared.

"Can I become small and tiny?" I ask Ded Moroz.

"Hmm..." he ponders. "But that won't solve anything; sooner or later, retribution will catch up with you."

"Grandpa, but if she's good, she might be lucky, right?" the Snow Maiden suggests.

"Maybe," he nods. "But not right away... She did terrible things, granddaughter."

"Well, Grandpa!" the girl says, looking at him with pity.

He agrees, promising me another chance if I'm good. I nod, agreeing to be good, especially since I'm dying anyway. Suddenly, everything around me fades away, and so do I...

---

* Russian name of Santa Claus. Since in Russia the "main" holiday is New Year's Eve, and not Christmas, as it was historically, but the functions of the Russian Father Christmas are broader - he can punish, freeze, and make a miracle

HOSPITAL

YOUNGER

My name is Mashenka, and I'm six years old. Right now, I'm in the hospital, but I'm not sure how I got here. I think I fell down at daycare. All I remember is suddenly feeling very hot in my tummy, and that's it, nothing else. I have a mom, a dad, and a grandpa, because my grandma passed away. Grandpa is my mom's dad, and my dad's parents never had a grandma or grandpa. I also have an aunt named Taisia, who's like a fairy godmother to me. Well, she's just a godmother, but I like to pretend she's a fairy. And Uncle Seryozha is my godfather, but he lives far away because he's a children's doctor.

When I open my eyes, I realize I'm not in a garden at all; everything around me is white and green. Something is beeping, and it's really interesting! There are flashing lights and lots of activity. I want to jump up and take a closer look, but I can't for some reason. I feel scared, so I start crying. Then, some men and women in light blue clothes rush into the room, where there are so many fascinating things. They all look the same in their shirts and trousers, so it's hard to tell who's who.

"Are you scared, little girl?" one of the women asks me.

"Yes," I reply, stopping my tears because I know the adults will help me. "I want my mom!"

"Don't worry, Mom and Dad are on their way," the woman reassures me. "Just lie down for a bit, okay?"

"Okay," I nod, realizing I have to do as I'm told. It feels like a game. "Am I being obedient?"

"You're the most obedient girl," the woman smiles at me. "Try to get some sleep."

I obediently close my eyes, but I'm too curious to sleep. I try to eavesdrop on what the ladies and gentlemen are doing and talking about, but it all sounds like gibberish to me. What's "o-ka-es"? And why is that man shaking his head and saying it doesn't work like that? It's interesting to listen in, but I quickly get tired and fall asleep.

I have a really scary dream. In it, I'm being very bad - hitting other girls and boys and hurting them in different ways. Even my mom and dad are hurting me. They're spanking me and pulling my hair. It's terrifying, so I wake up quickly and start crying because I'm scared!

"What's wrong, little one?" a plump woman rushes over to me. "Why are you crying?"

"I had a bad dream!" I tell her.

My aunt hugs me gently, which makes me feel less scared. She strokes my head, and I start to smile. She tucks me back in and asks me to be patient because Mom and Dad are coming.

And sure enough, my parents walk in. Mom cries and rushes over to hug me. I start crying too, so she won't be sad alone. We cry together until a stern nurse comes in and says we can't cry because it might upset my heart. Mom stops crying right away, and so do I, because it's no fun to cry alone. But I'm still confused about what's going on.

"When are we going home?" I ask Mom.

"We'll go home as soon as the doctors say it's okay," she tells me. "But for now, you have to stay here."

"But I don't want to be alone!" I start to whimper, but the doctor reassures me that Mom will stay with me so I won't be lonely.

"I'll stay with you, sweetie," Mom smiles at me.

I reach out to Dad too, because I can see he's about to cry too. I hug him and stroke him, and he smiles instead of crying. It's great when Dad smiles; it makes me happy. The doctors seem happy too, though I'm not sure why, but I don't ask questions so I don't bother them. Dad leaves with his phone in hand.

"Sergei will be here tonight," he tells Mom. "There are no

tickets for the next one, but he says he'll be here no matter what. Taisia is away on a business trip, so..."

"The main thing is Uncle Seryozha will come," Mom explains to me. "He's a doctor and will figure out what happened to our princess."

"Yay!" I'm happy because I love Uncle Seryozha.

I believe my godfather will come and everything will be fine because he's a doctor and knows everything. Maybe even more than Mom! Meanwhile, a nurse brings me some food, which is perfect timing because I skipped lunch at daycare, but I'm hungry. Mom helps me eat since my hands aren't moving well. She calls me all sorts of names like princess, darling, and daddy's miracle. So, I obediently eat some soup, even though it's not very tasty. I would refuse, but I'm hungry, and Mom says it's good for me. Dad hugs and kisses me some more, then rushes off to work because he has an important job.

After eating, I feel tired again, so I ask Mom to lie down next to me because I'm scared of having bad dreams. The doctor says I might have nightmares after this "o-ka-es," so Mom promises not to leave my side. She lies down on the cot next to mine, cuddles me, strokes me, and sings me a song. The song helps me drift off to sleep.

In my dream, I'm moving around, but not on my own legs. Instead, I'm in a special stroller. There are so many fascinating things around! Birds are singing, the breeze is gentle, and the sun is shining. Even though I can't walk in this dream, at least I'm not a naughty girl who deserves to be punished, even though I've never actually been punished. Mom has threatened to spank me a few times if I scatter my toys, but I'm a well-behaved girl. I try my best to remember to pick up my toys, but sometimes I forget. Then I start crying, and Mom forgets about the spanking because she has to comfort me, right?

"I hear Uncle Seryozha's voice as soon as I wake up, and it's very familiar," I think to myself. "Yay! Uncle Seryozha!" I exclaim happily and open my eyes.

Uncle Seryozha smiles warmly at me. He's dressed like the doctors here, focusing on something else before sitting down beside me. I immediately go in for a hug, feeling pleased to see him, and he reciprocates kindly. I wonder what's bothering him, but I'm determined to be an obedient girl.

"Hey there, Button," he begins, looking me straight in the eye. "What happened at daycare?"

"I don't remember much," I reply honestly. "I just remember feeling really hot here," I say, pointing to my tummy.

"Yeah," he nods, pulling out a stethoscope to listen to my

heartbeat. "It's quite unusual. How long did the episode last?"

"Almost a minute, colleague," another person responds, whom I didn't notice at first. "And there don't seem to be any aftereffects, although there should be."

"I can't hear any complications," my godfather remarks. "Let's have her under my supervision tomorrow, so she can stay home for a bit."

"But, Sergei..." Mom starts to say something, but stops for some reason.

"I'll stay with Button," Uncle Seryozha assures her. "So you can focus on your work."

"Thank you..." Mom begins to cry for some reason, and I consider joining her to keep her company. But Uncle Seryozha explains that Mom is just emotional and I shouldn't worry because I don't have any emotions yet.

"Crying for no reason isn't good for you," my godfather adds sternly, and I nod in agreement.

I realize that I'll probably get to go home tomorrow, back to my toys that I miss dearly. But for today, I'll have to stay put, as Uncle Seryozha instructed. Since it's already evening, I'll only have to spend one more night at the hospital before heading home. I nod in understanding and share my scary or sad dreams with Uncle Seryozha. He comforts me, assuring me that everything will be alright. I trust him because he's Uncle Seryozha.

"Now the little one will eat," Mom says affectionately.

"Then she'll sleep again, and before you know it, it'll be morning, right?"

"Okay," I agree, because I'm obedient, and no one asked me.

Mom can get quite angry, especially when she threatens to spank you, even though she never actually does. But I don't want to test it out. It's better to be obedient and avoid making anyone angry. Making Mom angry is definitely not a good idea, right? Uncle Seryozha also thinks it's best not to upset anyone and encourages me to be an obedient girl. Obedient girls usually get rewarded, but today I won't get any treats because I did something wrong at daycare. So, I eat the food I'm given. I can do it on my own! The food tastes bland, unlike Mom's cooking, which I tell her right away, and she smiles. During dinner, Dad arrives, but he smells different, which I notice right away. I don't say anything though, in case he accidentally spilled something on himself at work. He seems worried, after all.

They carry me to the bathroom so I don't have to exert myself. It's quite amusing, and I giggle, but I still brush my teeth as I should. Then, they tuck me back into bed. I still feel a bit jumpy from the day's events, so I quickly drift off to sleep.

In my dream, I'm the same troublesome girl, but now I'm furious because I just got in trouble myself. Instead of crying, I have the urge to hurt another girl for some reason. I don't understand why, but the desire is there, almost like craving candy. I even want to undress her, which is confusing. I try to stop myself in the dream, but I end up crying and waking up.

Mom isn't there, and I start crying even harder out of fear. But then I hear Mom's voice, so I listen intently through my tears. Mom says something cryptic about someone else having someone else for sure and someone is going to leave someone else somewhere soon. Listening is more engaging than crying, and besides, if I can hear Mom, she's nearby. I continue listening until I suddenly fall asleep again. This time, there's a girl in front of me, sharing her life story. She talks about being unloved, hurt, and mistreated as a child. I realize that's why she's angry - she wasn't loved. Then she tells me that I'm her, but I'm not as bad! I'm a good girl!

"What's wrong?" Mom wakes me up, and I just cry because I'm scared of being so bad.

"The child has nightmares," Uncle Seryozha notes, still by my side. "It happens after an incident like hers. We'll need to question her carefully, no matter how much she protests."

"Am I a good girl?" I ask, feeling anxious after my bad dream.

Maybe it's right that they punished me there because I needed it... But I had to stand in the corner and think, and it hurt so much there, even more than when Lisa pinches herself in kindergarten! But I don't learn from it, and I don't want to be good, just angry. I wonder, if I got punished, would I still be angry? I don't want to be...

"You're the best girl," Mummy says with a smile, and I

realize I don't need to be punished anymore; I'm already good!

I smile back, Mummy hugs me, and I fall asleep until morning. I don't dream about anything, not even that mean girl. Maybe where she comes from, they give good girls a smack on the butt instead of putting them in the corner. I don't want to be in a place like that! Can I stay with Mummy and Daddy instead of going back to that scary place where I'm mean?

I think they show me those dreams to remind me to be obedient and good, not like that girl, even though she said I was her. But Mummy confirmed I'm good! So I won't be like her... And you don't need to be scared, even though I am very, very scared of those dreams. If I met that girl, I'd probably be terrified! She's really, really scary!

I wake up without fear because Mummy and Uncle Seryozha are beside me. Daddy has already gone to work to provide for us. And soon, I'll go home, back to where I belong.

SISTERS-IN-DREAM

YOUNGER

I'm at home with Uncle Seryozha because both Mom and Dad are at work. It's nearly summer, and soon I'll be starting school in the fall. I used to feel excited about it, but now I'm a bit nervous. What if it's like that dream with the mean girl? But I try to be brave because I know Mom, Dad, and Uncle Seryozha will protect me. He's my godfather, after all.

Throughout the day, I play with dolls, watch TV, read with Uncle Seryozha, and listen to his fairy tales. He knows so many stories! It's really nice, and I never get bored. We also go to the playground, which I love. During the day, I don't remember my dreams, but sometimes I talk with the girl from my dreams. We try to figure out what went wrong together.

She listens to me, even though she's older, but she seems lost. I know how to do things right, but she doesn't, even though she's older. That's why we argue and cry together. She doesn't have parents like I do. They left her when she got sick. Sometimes I imagine what it would be like if I were abandoned because I was sick, and it scares me so much I wake Uncle Seryozha up at night.

"We're discussing a case I saw with the girl," I explain to her. "You got mad and hit a girl just because she said your underwear was showing. Why did you hit her without even checking?"

"She was trying to insult me," the girl, who's also named Masha like me, explains.

But I don't understand. You should always check first. What's so scary about showing your underwear? Maybe the boy had never seen it before and was curious. Why get upset about it? We agree that Masha will try to be kinder because being mean hurts her, and why should it hurt?

I feel better now because I don't have scary dreams anymore, but I still talk to Masha because she has no one else. So now she has me, and that feels right. She calls me sister, and I call her sister too because our names are the same, and it's easy to get confused. So now I have a dream sister. I hug her, and she smiles, and it's nice.

Some time passes, and sometimes I accidentally call Uncle Seryozha "Papa Seryozha" when Dad isn't around because he doesn't like it. My godfather checks me at the hospital again, but everything is fine. He smiles and has to leave. They let me go back to kindergarten.

At kindergarten, we have lessons and play games. I'm in the preparatory group because I'm getting older. Every morning, Mom takes me to kindergarten, even though I could go by myself. She's scared of bad people who might try to take me. Dream sister says there are bad people out there, so Mom is right to be cautious.

I feel sorry for my dream sister, so I tell her about my day. We sit together, and I tell her everything. Sometimes she smiles, and sometimes she cries because she never had that. She was in a bad girls' kindergarten. But who decided she was bad? It's strange how adults think sometimes. First, they put her in a bad place, and then they're surprised she acts out.

My parents knew right away that I was good, so I go to a kindergarten for good kids. We play and learn, but they don't teach us how to write yet. The teacher says we'll learn that later in school. I trust her, so I'll wait.

But guess what! I'm turning seven soon! It's a big celebration—my birthday, Mom says. Daddy agrees because I was very long-awaited. I wake up feeling excited. I also feel sorry for my dream sister because she never had a birthday. So we agree to celebrate hers today and mine in our dreams when I fall asleep.

I open one eye and see Mom looking at me mischievously. That means there's a surprise coming. I sit up, and Dad appears behind me. He lifts me up, and I laugh happily.

"Happy birthday, my daughter!" my parents say. "Grow big and strong!"

I promise I will because how could I not? Then we have a special breakfast and lots of presents—for school, pretty dresses, dolls, and even a dollhouse from Uncle Seryozha. He couldn't come today but will call later. And my fairy godmother will come visit when we get back from the park.

We have a big day ahead, with trips to the park, the zoo, and lunch at a restaurant. Mom and Dad take the day off to spend with me. It's wonderful! We watch a children's movie together in the evening, and then they tuck me into bed because I'm so happy happy happy!

But today is even more special because it's my dream sister's birthday too, and we'll celebrate together in our dreams.

Summer is finally here, and it's scorching hot! Mom told me we're going on vacation to the seaside this year, which is super exciting! I've been getting ready for it ahead of time, and guess what? Uncle Seryozha is sending me a swimsuit! Not just any swimsuit, but a full one, like the grown-ups wear! It's blue with green and flowery patterns, and I absolutely love it! Aunt Taisia gave me a lovely airy dress that goes perfectly with my swimsuit, according to Mom. Even my dream sister was amazed because she's never had one. She almost cried, but I hugged her, and she decided not to because she was happy with me.

All week, I've been eagerly waiting for our trip, bombarding my parents with questions. Mom is very patient; she tells me all about the train ride and even shows me a picture. I'm buzzing with excitement! I've already packed my underwear, shirts, shorts, and even my dolls and teddy bear. My rucksack looks like a ladybug with antennas—yellow instead of red—but still very pretty! Folding everything neatly has been keeping me busy all week. The bear doesn't fit properly, but I refuse to leave it behind. We'll be traveling for a long time, even sleeping on the train, before finally reaching the sea! My sister is also very curious about the sea.

The week goes by slowly, but finally, departure day arrives. I've been eagerly waiting since morning to head to the station. Mom and Dad are still packing and doing other things, but they ask me to wait in my room, and I do because I'm an obedient and very good girl.

"Mashenka, are you ready?" Mom asks when she enters the room.

"Yes, Mommy," I answer from my highchair, snuggled up with the dog.

Matilda, the dog, stays at home because she won't fit in my rucksack. But we agreed she'd wait for me without feeling offended. She's very good; she can bark and follow commands in German, thanks to Uncle Seryozha. But I already know all those words and many more.

"Come on, sweetie," Mom says softly, and I jump up from my chair, almost forgetting my rucksack.

"Hooray! The sea!" I shout with joy, but Mom just smiles.

Daddy is smiling too, despite having two big suitcases. Downstairs, a car is waiting for us. Daddy called a taxi to take us to the station. We quickly get inside, and the taxi pulls away. I look out the window, waving goodbye to our home. We'll be back in almost a month when my parents' vacation is over, but right now, the train station awaits us! I've been there before, but I don't remember because of that incident in kindergarten, when I was in the hospital. I forgot everything! But now I get to experience it all again!

The station is big and full of interesting things, but Mom holds my hand tightly, not letting me get distracted by the beautiful sights. That's probably why we quickly find our way to our train carriage. Dad hands something to a man in a cap who smiles at me and gestures towards our carriage. I realize it's huge! Inside, there's a long corridor with doors, and we enter one of them. There's a sofa, an armchair, a TV set, I think, and another door.

"Did you book a suite?" Mom asks, surprised. "That's expensive!"

"It's a holiday, darling," Dad replies, arranging things on the shelf. "We're traveling in style. And the princess will sleep with you anyway... Or with me, so she doesn't fall off."

"Thank you," Mom says quietly, kissing Dad on the lips.

"Let's sit down," Dad suggests.

Mom sits me down, and I take out my teddy bear from my rucksack to play with during the journey. I sit by the window, showing Ted—the bear—everything outside, and explaining it all. Mom giggles for some reason, but maybe she's just happy because we're leaving soon. And when I think that, the carriage lurches, and the station starts to move backward. People, poles, signs—everything passes by as we begin our journey!

As the railway station fades away, the city begins. It speeds up, and I look out the window with Ted. He looks a lot like the bear in the cartoon, hence the name. I show him everything, imagining my little sister is seeing it all too because she's interested!

Then Mom says it's time to eat, and I find out there's a place to wash my hands right here in our room. Dad helps me wash my hands while Mom sets out our meal. It smells delicious, just like Mom's cooking always does. So it's homemade, not store-bought. I tell her I prefer her cooking, and she smiles. It's so nice when Mom smiles, I can't explain!

The porridge and chicken are delicious, so I eat them eagerly. Mom even thought of Ted, so he gets porridge too. It's a toy, but it's there! Mom is very, very caring! And since it's tasty and I'm obedient, I finish it all and get a little cake as a treat.

I'm not bored at all during the journey because Ted is there. We play, I tell him everything, and I give him hugs too. Mom says I need to rest a bit after eating, and I agree because I'm feeling sleepy. So I take off my dress to avoid wrinkling it in my sleep, and I'm left in just my underwear. Mom puts me on the sofa, making sure I'm comfortable, I cuddle my bear, and she strokes me until I fall asleep quickly.

"Thank you, thank you, thank you, thank you!" my dream sister says as she hugs me in my sleep.

"You saw it, right?" I ask her, and she nods.

"I saw..." She looks like she wants to cry, but she doesn't; she just hugs me. "Thank you!"

I feel a bit embarrassed and tell her she's welcome because she's my little sister. I need to remember that if I want to show something to my little sister when I'm awake, she can see it and be happy with me. She's completely forgotten about her sadness and is acting almost like me. That's very, very good!

THE SEA

YOUNGER

The sea... It's amazing! It's beyond words!

We arrive early in the morning, but I don't mind being woken up because it's the sea! Daddy says we need to check in first, so another taxi picks us up from the station, and we settle in. While Daddy takes care of some paperwork, Mom and I head up to the room. It's like a flat, but smaller and without a kitchen. Ted and I will stay in one room, and Mom and Dad will be in the other.

"This is where we'll stay," Mom tells me. "Well, what are you waiting for? Get changed!"

"Yay!" I exclaim and rush into the room with my rucksack to change into my swimsuit. I can do it here!

Once I'm all set, Mom tells me to put on the dress my fairy godmother gave me. I nod and put it on because Mom said so! Mom and Dad can't be wrong, so I trust them. And with a panama hat, of course, we're ready to hit the beach!

"What's the dress for?" I ask Mom.

"It's for when you're done swimming," she explains. "You can't walk around with just your swimsuit on."

I nod and hand her my panties too, and she smiles at me. So I got it right! I need a dress too, I'll look very pretty in it, and everyone will admire me. Mom says a girl should be admired because it's the right thing to do. If it's right, then let them admire me, no problem!

Mom takes my hand, and we head downstairs where Daddy is waiting. I give him my other hand, and we stroll down the street—Mom, Dad, and me! It's sunny, and there are some unusual trees Daddy calls "palm trees." I try to remember, and I also try to show everything to my little sister so she can see it too.

There are lots of people around, but I'm not scared. I just walk and look around until we reach the beach. There are even more people here, lots of sand, and it's the sea! It's hard to describe, but it's blue-green, smells like seaweed, and just feels extraordinary.

I jump in, and Mom helps me swim, although I know how to swim. She keeps me safe, and I'm just happy because it's fantastic! After a while, I get out to play in the sand before going back into the sea. Mom says we won't change into dry clothes yet, and I notice lots of girls and boys running around without panties. But Daddy... Uncle Seryozha said it's not right! It's bad for peeing because sand can get in there. But no one listens to me, so I just build a sandcastle and then back into the water.

The time until lunch flies by quickly, but I'm not upset because I'm on vacation. At lunchtime, Mom says it's time to eat, so off we go. Mom also hands me my panties, and I understand—I have to change out of my wet swimsuit. It's a bit hard to take it off because it's wet, but Mom helps me change. I'm not embarrassed because there are lots of kids running around without clothes, so I'm just changing. My little sister says they're usually shy about being in public without clothes, but I don't see why they should be, so I'm not.

"What are we eating?" I ask because there's no kitchen.

"You'll see," Mom smiles at me and leads the way.

I'm very curious, and I notice both Mom and Dad are smiling today. Mom holds my hand, Dad hugs her, and she's glowing. It's beautiful to see, well, I think so because they're my parents. If it makes them happy, it makes me happy too. We enter a café with tables outside and inside. It's cooler inside, so Mom decides to stay there.

A waiter hands us menus with words and pictures. I start looking closer while Dad talks to the waiter. Then they bring me juice in a tall glass, and Mom and Dad get something else, but I don't know what because their glasses are different shapes. Mom tells me to wait, and I focus on the interesting menu. I already know the letters, so I try to read it.

I read "pizza" and "pasta," and I want to read more, but then the food arrives. It's round, like bread, on a big plate. Dad starts teaching me how to eat the pizza properly so I don't make a mess, but I still spill some. I don't get upset, and neither does Mom because we're on vacation, and there's no need to. It's normal for kids like me.

Dad thinks so too, so we eat. The pizza is delicious, but it's huge, so I can't finish it all. Mom says I don't have to because we'll take it with us for dinner later. She's very clever, my Mom!

When I'm too full to eat anymore, Mom and Dad pay, and we get two square boxes. That's our dinner, Mom says. Now we're going back to the hotel, and later, we'll probably go back to the beach. We've come to the sea, so there's no reason to stay in the hotel...

"No, my daughter," Mom explains. "You need to rest after lunch. It's hot outside now, but in the evening..."

I already know about "quiet time" when kids like me aren't allowed out to avoid headaches. So it's better to stay in the hotel and watch cartoons on TV. I like cartoons a lot! That's why I'm not being naughty; I'm just going to watch... Well, first, I'll take a nap and share it with my little sister, and then we'll watch cartoons together because we're sisters!

My little sister greets me with tears, not because she's sad, but because she feels and sees the same things I do, and that makes her emotional. We're girls, so our emotions come out in tears—that's what Daddy... Uncle Seryozha says. So we hug and let our emotions out. My sister wants to cry, and I want to join her because she'll be lonely crying alone, right?

Holidays aren't just about sitting around! Daddy and Mommy are taking me to a water park! I don't know what it is yet, but I'm super interested because it sounds like so much fun! Mommy and Daddy hug because they love each other, Daddy explained to me. He said that when a boy and a girl grow up, they can like each other, and then love happens. Then, with that love, they get married and have children. I know that because I came out of my mom's tummy; she told me a long time ago.

Mommy and Daddy love each other, so they hug each other, and I love them too. Sometimes I ride on Daddy's neck, even though I'm getting heavy, but Daddy still carries me because he's Daddy. But now I walk beside them, looking around because there are so many interesting things! There's a monkey sitting on my uncle, eating a banana! There's a white car without a roof! And there's a kitty cat! Mommy just smiles when I show her, and Daddy smiles too.

The water park is huge, with five pools, many slides, swings, and merry-go-rounds in the water! And there are lots of kids! Mommy nods at me, and I rush towards the slides. Climbing up and then flying down a tube with holes in it is so exciting! I laugh as I splash into the water! I'm sure my little sister is laughing too because she can see everything!

"Hi, I'm Masha!" I bump into a girl in the water and introduce myself right away.

"Hi, I'm Ira!" The girl, who looked angry at first, smiles back. "Where do you live?"

We start chatting and find out that Ira lives very close to us in a hotel, so we can probably play together if our moms let us. Well, mine will let us, but I don't know about hers. We play together and have fun because it's the right thing to do. Then we go on the slide and the merry-go-round. Mommy notices that I have a new friend and goes to meet Ira's mom. Daddy brings them a drink because they're not falling down like us!

Mommy says that since we live nearby, we can visit and play, and now we have more "attractions." I try to pronounce the word correctly, but Ira does it better. But I'm not upset because sometimes someone does better than you, and that's okay, that's what the teacher says.

Then they take us to a café for lunch to eat delicious things. Daddy says he's treating us, but Ira's mom blushes for some reason. They bring us rice with something tasty inside, so Ira and I eat together. She lives far away in the north, where there are live reindeer running around, it's almost always snowing, and even bears! Daddy says we're in the "middle zone." We also have bears, but I haven't seen them, and Ira's mom says it's good that I haven't.

After lunch, we go back to the hotel because I need to sleep. For some reason, Ira doesn't, but we agree to meet in the evening on the beach to play together. In the meantime, I need to... but I don't get upset because I'm a good girl. I tuck myself into bed to share with my little sister. She's very happy, and happy that we're having such a great holiday. She also says that I am the best sister in the world, so we cuddle, and then it's time to wake up to go to the sea with Ira.

We play so much that we don't even notice when it's time to go to bed because it's late, even though it's light. But the next day, Mommy and Daddy take me to see the fish! It's such a big aquarium with many different fish swimming around. Daddy tells me about each fish. It turns out that there are not only those that people eat but also those that can eat people! I don't want to be eaten, so we stick to looking at the friendly ones. They're so cute! It's too bad we can't play with them.

Then Daddy takes me on a roundabout and a car ride. It's really fun to ride with other cars, bump into them, and get bumped back. I just laugh with joy because it's so interesting. Daddy also says we're going to the cinema, which is new. Well, not the cartoons themselves, but everything else is new! We're given special glasses, and it feels like I'm inside the cartoon, with the wind blowing and everything! And the water! It was so amazing, I can't describe it!

And it's like this every day! Every day is so interesting, fun, and joyful that I just can't tell you how much. I'm learning about "pizza" and discovering that pasta comes in many different shapes. And ice cream! It's different and delicious. Also, no one scolds me when I drool, but I do sometimes... well, it happens. I realize that I'm like a pig, but nobody scolds me, not even my sister. She strokes me and says that I'm the best. I like being the best because it's the right thing to do!

Mommy and Daddy smile all the time because they're happy too. And I'm happy not only because there's so much sea and games but also because Mommy and Daddy are happy. Their smiles make me happy too, and my little sister is happy too. I think she believes that we're sisters and we'll be together forever. I don't know why it happened, but it did. She didn't have anyone else, and now she has me, and Mommy and Daddy have me too, even though they don't know. I wanted to tell them, but my sister told me not to because we only meet in dreams, and adults won't understand. But I believe they will because they're parents.

And then, suddenly, the holiday ends, and we have to go back because school starts soon. At first, I want to cry, but my sister says that it always happens, and I decide not to cry, at least not while I'm awake. When I'm asleep, it's a different story. I say goodbye to Ira, promising to write to each other and meet again next year for sure! We hug and even shed a few tears, but not too many because we'll see each other again! Then Ira gets on a plane, and we have to go to the train...

THE DREADED BLACK SORCERER

YOUNGER

I'M STARTING SCHOOL TODAY! Isn't it exciting? I'm wearing a beautiful dress with a big bouquet of flowers for the teacher, and I have a satchel like everyone else. Mom says I'll be the prettiest girl today if I stay neat. So, I'm being careful not to mess up and look messy.

At school, all the kids are gathered, and they seem really happy, even though they don't know us yet. They give me a big bell to ring, and then an older boy lifts me onto his shoulders and we walk around the circle. I'm ringing the bell because I'm so happy. I'm giving the first bell myself!

After saying goodbye to Mom and Dad, I head to class for my first lesson. I'm trying hard to be a good girl today, very obedient and angelic, just like Dad says. I sit in class, sing songs, read syllables, and even count sticks, and the teacher praises me.

The first day goes by quickly, and when they let us out, I see Mom, Dad, and aunt Taisia! I run to them because I have so much to tell. I'm a first-grader now, and I'm really proud. I want to do well in school, get good grades, and make Mom and Dad proud!

Now I have homework, but it's not too hard. However, I can't go to P.E. with everyone else because Uncle Seryozha said it's too risky. Mom agrees, and so does Dad. Grandpa didn't seem happy about it, but Mom covered my ears. My little sister thinks Grandpa doesn't love me, but I'm not bothered. I know Mom and Dad love me, and that's enough.

I'm busy with school and homework, so I'm very tired, but I eat well and sleep well. Mom is teaching me how to use the microwave to heat my own food. It's not difficult, so I do it well. I walk to school by myself because it's close by, and I'm big enough to do it alone.

Mom praises me more and more, but I notice she smiles less, and Dad sometimes seems annoyed. I don't know why, but I don't make a fuss. My sister says it happens to adults, and my job is to study hard to make Mom and Dad happy.

Then, suddenly, it's autumn break, but it's only a week, so we stay home. I spend my time decorating notebooks and playing in the yard while Mom and Dad are at work.

One day, I see a fancy car pull up to our house, and Mom gets out with some man. I don't like him, but I don't say anything. I watch them hug and kiss, just like Mom and Dad do. It makes me feel weird and scared. What if that man is doing something bad to Mom? What if she's in danger?

The car leaves, and I quietly cry because I don't understand what's happening. Mom and Dad have love, right? But now it seems like Mom has been bewitched, like in a cartoon. Does that mean there's no love anymore? I'm scared to tell anyone what I saw because I don't want Mom or Dad to get hurt.

I go to our neighbor Miss Zina's house to wash my face, but she's not home. I decide to go back home and pretend everything is fine because I don't want Mom to be in danger. I'll do anything to protect her.

"Are you back, Mashenka?" Mom calls me. "Did you have a nice walk?"

"Yes, Mom," I reply, trying to sound cheerful even though I'm scared for her.

After washing up, I watch Mom closely. She seems cheerful, but her eyes don't look the same. She's really been bewitched. How do I undo the spell? Maybe I should ask my sister for advice.

I try to be cheerful for the rest of the evening so no one suspects anything. I think I'm doing okay because Dad still smiles at Mom, and Mom still smiles at Dad. They talk to me lovingly. I go to bed, eager to talk to my sister. She always knows what to do.

"You see, sis," she says, crying with me, "that's just how it is sometimes. You could tell Dad, but they'd probably just argue, and that would be it."

I talked to her more, and it turns out that sometimes "love" doesn't last forever, so there's no need to cry. You just keep living because the grown-ups will figure things out on their own. But I realize that the bad feelings won't just go away. If it comes down to it, I'd rather the bad stuff take me instead of Mom. She can have another daughter, but I don't have a brother, so it's okay if they take me. I love Mom so much that I'd even let myself be sacrificed for her. Evil sorcerers, they're like Baba Yaga, always after little girls because we're like treats to them. So if it means making Mom happy, I'll let them take me

I can only see the scary black sorcerer uncle in a couple of days because I have to make sure he doesn't harm Mom. So she has to go home, and I... I agree to switch places with Mom! So it's okay, but first, I have to go to school. Because the evil sorcerer brings Mom back in the afternoon, almost in the evening, and there's still school until then.

If it weren't for my little sister, I would probably cry day and night, but she hugs me and strengthens my decision to save Mom. My little sister doesn't discourage me; she just strokes me and tells me that I'm a good girl. It's good that I have her because without her, it would be very bad, and this way, I am not alone.

I go to school, even though my heart is sad, I know I should smile, and so I smile. I smile very big so that nobody knows how sad I am. So I smile, and I remember how great it was before Mom was bewitched. It makes me want to smile and cry at the same time. But I hold on because no one can deal with the scary black sorcerer but me.

Today must be a particularly bad day because when I go out to recess, some boy runs up behind me and pulls up my skirt. At first, I want to cry, then I want to hurt him, but I quickly pull myself together because I'm a good girl, and the boy is probably one of the bad ones, or maybe he's just curious about panties.

"Do you want to see the knickers?" I asked him. "You don't have any of your own, do you? So you've never seen them, and now you just want to see them?"

"You! I'm gonna get you now!" The bad boy swings at me, and I imagine he's just like a sissy, well, without affection all his life.

"Poor little thing," I said to him. "Don't worry, I won't tell anyone you don't have them."

"I'll get you!" He shouts, but then suddenly he turns and runs away, and I don't understand why he's doing this because I'm really not going to tell.

But the boy doesn't come back, and it seems that nobody

really heard us, then why did he run away? I don't understand these boys, really. I guess when they grow up, there's something in them that makes them like girls so they can marry and love. Until then, they're incomprehensible, like this boy. I sigh and walk back to the classroom because I'm not having fun.

The teacher noticed I wasn't happy, but she thought it was because of what the boy did. She told me I shouldn't be upset about it, and I said I wasn't upset because maybe he'd never seen knickers before. You can't get mad at someone who doesn't even have knickers. The teacher started to smile and then giggled, letting me go. But she giggles sometimes during class too; she probably got a chuckle in her mouth.

During lessons, I forced myself not to think about Mom being bewitched, even though I wanted to cry non-stop. But my sister says I'm strong, so I need to hold myself together. That's why I do well in class and get straight A's, to please her, I guess. Maybe Daddy will be happy at least, since Mom's under a spell for now.

When I come home, I change my clothes and warm up my lunch. For some reason, I find porridge unpalatable today, even though I used to like it a lot. But today it's tasteless, and I don't feel like doing anything - neither going out nor doing homework. So, after eating, I sit down to do my homework quickly so that I can finish and go out into the street. Maybe I'll be able to talk to the sorcerer because I'm tired of waiting... After quickly finishing my math and writing correctly, I go outside to hide and wait for the scary black sorcerer to bring my mommy.

I think I'm lucky today. I see that scary black car again, and Mom kisses the sorcerer with joy and runs away. For some reason, the scary uncle doesn't leave at once but starts sucking on a smoking pipe. It's a cigarette; I know it's terribly harmful, that's what Uncle Seryozha says, but the black sorcerer is probably allowed to because he's not sorry for it. I come out from around the corner and approach the scary man, even though I'm afraid and I need to go to the toilet.

"Are you trying to take my mommy away from me?" I ask him softly, causing the sorcerer to cough. "I agree; you can eat me, but just uncharm Mommy, please."

The scary black sorcerer throws away his cigarette and then squats down and looks me in the eyes. And I, stammering, tell him that mommy and daddy have "love" and that if anything, they will have another child, and he can eat me because Mommy is more important. Suddenly the man stops being scary. He reaches out and strokes my head.

"What are you doing, little girl?" the sorcerer shakes his head. "I would never take a mommy away from such a good girl. I'm sorry, I didn't know she was your mommy."

"Are you going to cast a spell on her?" I ask him. "You can do whatever you want to me!"

"I'm not going to do anything, baby," he smiles sadly.

"And I'm going to uncharm your mom right now, only she won't like it; she might get angry, do you understand?"

"Let it go," I decide, because it really does. "As long as she wasn't bewitched..."

"Okay," he smiles at me. "You run home, and I'll do your mom's magic."

And I believe him! So I run home with joyful anticipation, like a birthday right before a birthday. I'm running home to see Mom get a new Mommy and become the same Mommy. I really, really want to see it because it's Mommy! I believe the scary black sorcerer; for some reason, I believe him very much, and I run with all my legs. Mommy's going to be the same!

I nearly fall over, just running and running, not even thinking about how Mommy would react to being abruptly split open. Out of breath, I run up to the door to unlock it. Not immediately getting my key into the keyhole, I open the door abruptly and run into the house. I don't hear anything at first, so I throw off my street jacket and shoes and run into the room.

"Mommy! Mommy, I'm home!" I shout happily and then falter.

Some stranger's mom is looking at me. Her eyes are in tears, but that's not the main thing; she's looking at me like she wants to beat me up or something. It's so scary, just creepy like that, and then she gets up abruptly from the couch and steps towards me with a very angry face, raising her hand for something. But what she wants to do, I don't understand because suddenly the lights go out, and my little sister grabs me, pulling me against her.

WHO LOVES TEARS

YOUNGER

My little sister comforts me by saying that the uncle probably "sent" Mommy away, and that's why she was angry. But then I suddenly fell asleep and startled everyone, because it's Mommy, and you have to believe she's good. I believe very, very much. My little sister strokes me and assures me that everything will be better because the scary uncle turned out not to be bad. And then I wake up.

Everything around me is white, and something is beeping to my left. So I'm back in the hospital. There's a doctor next to me, wearing a green suit. He's frowning and looking at something on a paper. When he sees that I am awake, the doctor strokes my head and immediately smiles kindly.

"Are you awake, my good girl?" he asks me softly. "What were you so scared of?"

"I don't remember," I answer honestly, because I really don't. The whole day is a blur; I don't even remember what happened at school. I just remember talking to my sister, but now it's all hazy. All I know is that an evil sorcerer has cast a spell on my mom. I don't know anything else.

"It's okay, it happens," the doctor reassures me, smiling. "Now we'll call your mom to show you that you're alive."

For some reason, I feel a little scared, but I force myself not to be afraid because I'm in a hospital, so everything will be fine. Why did I fall asleep? It had something to do with Mommy, I think. But then the door opens, and Mommy comes running into the room. Not bewitched! Just scared, I think. She rushes to me, immediately hugging me.

"Masha, my daughter, you scared me so much!" exclaims Mommy. "I already thought... I thought..."

"I love you so much, Mommy!" I tell her, and she pulls me close to her.

"My baby," Mommy says, stroking me. "Don't be so frightened, Mommy loves you very, very much too."

"I won't do it again," I promise her, though I'm not sure I can keep that promise.

The doctor comes in, explains something to Mommy, she nods, not letting me out of her arms, and then it turns out that they are sending me home. Well, because everything has been cleared up, and I'll stay at home with my mommy for a couple more days to make sure everything is okay, and then I'll go back to school. Turns out you can't scare me because my heart doesn't like it. I don't like it either, but I don't remember what I was scared of, and the doctor said that it happens, and my mom said so too. And in the evening, when we were already home, Uncle Seryozha said "aha," and I didn't hear the rest, but we are not home yet.

Mommy carried me in her arms, even though I was heavy, but she was very scared. She was so scared that she just clutched me to her chest. She goes out into the street, and just then a car pulls up, which I immediately recognize - it's Daddy! He doesn't have a long scary car like the witch doctor, so I start smiling right away.

"I'm sorry, darling, I came as soon as I could," Dad jumps out of the car, but Mom won't let him have me. "What's wrong?"

"Mashenka fainted," Mommy says in a crying voice, and Daddy immediately hugs her.

They put me in the seat, and my parents calm down. Well, in their own way, I mean they hug and smooch, but I'm glad they do because a mommy hugging a sorcerer is very scary. So I smile happily because Mommy is real again and not bewitched. And the sorcerer turned out to be good, though scary, it turns out, only I don't remember how it was....

We're driving home, and I'm smiling while Mummy tells Daddy that I shouldn't be scared because my heart might fail, causing me to faint unexpectedly. But I'm not afraid because in my dreams, my little sister is always there, and she's very good and not scary at all. Daddy shakes his head and reassures me that I shouldn't worry because nothing bad can happen.

Then we arrive home and have dinner. Mummy sighs for some reason, but she doesn't say why, and the house is a bit messy because she cleaned everything when she got scared. I want to help her tidy up, but Mummy insists that I lie down, so I obey. Daddy suggests he'll inform the teacher that I won't be at school, but Mummy says it's unnecessary because the hospital already called to ensure I don't get frightened. Daddy smiles and announces he's ready to eat.

Mummy nods and heads to the kitchen to cook while I happily watch cartoons Daddy put on for me. They're very funny, and I have time to think because everyone is occupied and not paying attention to me. I wonder if I somehow defeated the evil sorcerer, but I realize I probably didn't have the strength. I'll have to ask my sister how I did it. But for now, it's time to eat!

I don't even notice how the day ends. Mummy prepares a delicious dinner, and Daddy and I praise her, making her smile, albeit a little sadly. I'm not sure why she's sad, but I figure adults can have different thoughts, so as long as she's smiling, it's good.

Tonight, Mummy washes me, except for one spot, because Uncle Seryozha said it's best to keep that area clean with fewer hands touching it. Mummy agrees, and after washing, she tucks me into bed, strokes my head, and tells me a bedtime story. So I fall asleep, knowing I don't have school tomorrow, but obedience demands I sleep nonetheless!

My little sister hugs me tightly. She knows I don't remember what happened, but she starts recounting how I convinced the scary sorcerer to release my mom. He turned out not to be bad, even though he was a sorcerer, and once he realized my mom was involved, he immediately freed her.

"So Mom might have been angry because he freed her too quickly," I reason.

My sister tells me about people who drink from a bottle and can get angry if it's taken away abruptly. I suppose that's what Mom wanted to avoid. It's scary when someone wants to harm you, and my sister's description of it terrifies me, so I hope to never experience it.

I'm doing really well in school, and the New Year is almost here! But lately, Mom and Dad have been arguing more loudly, and Mom ends up crying. At first, I thought they were just having a disagreement, but I realized that arguing is bad, and Mom and Dad shouldn't do things that are bad. When I tell my little sister stories, she just comforts me by stroking me.

Once, I thought their argument was because of something I did, although I wasn't sure what. Maybe they were deciding how to punish me, like taking away sweets or TV time. But I didn't want to argue, so I decided I'd rather be spanked. I did what my sister said she'd do—I brought Dad's strap to them. But instead of spanking me, they argued even more. Maybe they couldn't decide how to handle it. Mom hugged me and cried, probably because she lost the argument again.

So when my parents argue, I go to my room to avoid bothering them. If that's what they want, I'll leave them be, but it makes me feel like crying for some reason. Thankfully, my little sister calms me down. When I'm not at school, I spend a lot of time sleeping, especially with her, because being with her makes me feel better.

When it snows, my parents and I go sledding, but not always together. Sometimes I worry they're pushing themselves too hard, but my sister says not to think like that. She's really smart. Otherwise, I'd probably cry a lot more, especially during the day when I'm scared because Mom argues really loudly.

Despite everything, I try to stay happy about the snow because New Year's Eve is almost here! Santa Claus will come and bring presents. I already know what I'll ask him for, but it's a secret! In the meantime, I go sledding with Dad, and while Mom doesn't always join us, I make sure she's okay. She's not herself lately, so I help out more around the house, like cleaning and using the vacuum. I'm not allowed in the kitchen, though.

Dad brings home the Christmas tree, and its smell makes

me even happier because everything will be okay. On Sunday, we decorate the tree together—Dad, Mom, and me. I put the ornaments up high and low, and Dad lifts me so I can place the star on top. It lights up with colorful lights, which is so cool! It means Christmas is almost here!

And then Santa Claus visits! I wrote a poem for him, and he smiles as I read it. He looks a bit like Dad, but I know it can't be him because he's at work. Finally, it's time for what I've been waiting for!

"What would you like?" Ded Moroz ponders. "A bunny or a doll?"

"Don't give me anything, Ded Moroz," I request. "Just ensure that Mommy and Daddy stop arguing and stay together!"

"Okay, dear," he responds in a gentle tone, then walks away. Will he fulfill my request?

"My little one!" Mommy cries, embracing me tightly, nearly squeezing my bones.

When Dad returns from work, he smells like a Christmas tree, but there's also a faint scent of medicine. I don't recall it being this way before, so it must be different now. I'm happy that Mommy and Daddy argue less, although I still hear them sometimes, but I don't cry anymore, well, not often...

Then Dad goes out for work all night, leaving Mommy unhappy because she has to watch over me. I can hear her talking to someone on the phone. After she finishes, I suggest she go with Dad and leave me alone since I'm big enough.

This makes Mommy angry, warning me of consequences if I interfere. It surprises me, but I remember what my sister said, so I agree and want to leave, because upsetting adults when they're upset isn't good. That's what sis says. But apparently, I say the wrong thing because Mommy gets even angrier and puts me on her lap with my tummy.

I'm unsure of what she intends or why she's removing my underwear. Suddenly, there's a sharp sting on my bottom, and I find myself in my little sister's arms. She hugs me, crying, and I hug her back, wiping her tears and asking why she's crying. Sis explains that Mommy was spanking me, but since I got scared, I'm back with her. I nod, suggesting I should wake up again because Mommy is trying, and I should cry to make her feel better, so her effort isn't wasted.

I wake up to find myself on the bed, with Mommy hugging me, asking me to open my eyes. I tell Mommy not to cry because my dress is already wet. Mommy spanked me, and I fell asleep, and she thought I died from it. I promise Mommy I'll try not to fall asleep next time, and if she wants to spank me again, I'll cry to make her feel better.

"Do you think it pleases me to see you crying?" Mom asks softly.

"You're hurting my bottom," I explain. "If it hurts, then I cry, so you want me to cry, right? And if I'm asleep, I'm not crying, and that makes you sad."

"Baby..." Mom starts crying as if I kicked her bottom. "I'll never... I swear... Never again!"

"Don't cry, Mommy," I comfort her and stroke her, feeling like crying too because Mommy is crying...

Mommy hugs me and vows never to spank my bottom again because she doesn't like my tears. If she doesn't like it, then why did she spank me? Sometimes, I don't understand parents. But the important thing is that Mommy stops crying because it's sad when she cries.

Mommy tucks me into bed, and in my dream, I sit with my little sister, telling her what happened. She praises me and strokes me. I love it when she strokes me because she's my little sister! We chat, and when I wake up in the morning, Daddy is there, but Mommy doesn't seem pleased because Daddy was "drunk" and wet himself. I thought big uncles didn't do that, but apparently, it happens. When Daddy wakes up, Mommy sends me out to sled in the yard, forgetting that the windows open, so I can hear their argument. It's quite interesting! Daddy brought Mommy a present in his pocket—panties—but Mommy didn't like them. Funny how adults can be sometimes...

ACCIDENT

YOUNGER

Despite the strange moments and arguments, New Year's Eve is really joyful, and I even receive presents, though I know they're not from Santa Claus because that's not what I asked for. After all the celebrations, fireworks, and happiness, when Dad is tucking me into bed, he says something odd about leaving one day. I didn't quite grasp what he meant, but I was too thrilled about New Year's Eve to dwell on it!

"Do you understand what Daddy meant?" I ask my little sister while half asleep.

. . .

Her eyes fill with sadness, and she tries to explain, but I struggle to comprehend. Then it hits me. Sometimes adults have to take a long journey away from home, like a walk, for a really long time, even a whole year. Daddy warned me about this so I wouldn't be scared or cry. He's so considerate! Now I know that even if he goes away, he'll come back someday, so I just need to wait.

Adults are so complex; you never quite know what they're thinking. But I'm just a little girl, and luckily, I have my little sister to explain things to me, so I'm not afraid at all. By the way, in my dream, I created a room exactly like mine, even with a crib, although my little sister says she doesn't need to sleep. But how could I not have a crib?

Now my little sister lives in my dream room. We have toys, games, and books she can read. I'm not sure how it works, but sis says it's very cozy. So when I close my eyes, I'm in my room with my little sister waiting for me. It's wonderful!

After New Year's Eve, things aren't as exciting, even though I've been chosen as Head Girl at school! That means I have to be in charge and keep things in order. But there's not much to keep in order because everyone is good, except for Valera. He bullies others, especially girls, but my sister says we should try to talk to him because he might be lonely like her. She even teaches me how to talk to a boy like her. And I follow her advice.

"Let's step back," I say calmly to Valera.

"Come on," he smiles wickedly, but I can see the longing in his eyes, similar to what my little sister expressed to me.

We move away from the others, and right away, I extend friendship to him. Without waiting for his response, I mention that he seems sad, evident from his demeanor. I gently stroke his arm, and he struggles to hold back tears. It's clear that Valera is on the verge of crying, so I embrace him like a caring sister and ask what's troubling him. We shed a few tears together, but I reassure him that we're friends, and he manages a smile.

Valera's mom is terminally ill... She might have a month or maybe six left, but her condition is irreversible. In the evening, I ask my mom to contact Uncle Seryozha to inquire about it. Unfortunately, there's no hope for her, as confirmed by my godfather, but he advises me to speak to the teacher and emphasize that Valera needs support because it's a frightening experience. The mere thought of it nearly makes me doze off on the spot.

As time passes and winter fades, I notice a change in Daddy's behavior, as if he's under a spell. However, I don't see any sorcerer around, so I question Mom if Daddy has been enchanted, like she seems to be. Mom breaks down in tears, expressing that she'd rather be bewitched because Daddy's behavior has become difficult to handle. It's puzzling because Daddy can't be bad; after all, he's Daddy. Mom must have misunderstood something.

And then Daddy arrives... it's Uncle Seryozha! I'm overjoyed to see him, nearly bursting with excitement. He lifts me up, despite my weight, and I giggle with delight. My godfather brings my toys and then goes to have a discussion with my parents. I know it's not right to eavesdrop, so I resist the urge, even though I'm intensely curious. When he emerges, he sighs and remarks that I'm the only one acting normal. I don't quite grasp the implication, so I express my confusion to him.

"Let's hope your mum and dad remember that they are adults," Uncle Seryozha responds to me.

"Do they think they're babies?" I ponder aloud.

My godfather simply gives me a comforting hug, and I contemplate. If Mommy and Daddy are behaving like babies, it would make sense! Maybe they just need to relearn how to use the potty, or perhaps they need a babysitter before they make a mess! I share my thoughts with Uncle Seryozha, who chuckles and reassures me that Mommy and Daddy will reflect on their actions now that they've been put in their place.

Then we go for a walk with Pa... Uncle Seryozha. Well, Mommy and Daddy are grounded, so we stroll together. He shares stories about his sweetheart and his daughter, even mentioning that one day they'll visit too. But his daughter can't come just yet—she's tied up with school, you know how it is. I listen intently, feeling glad that my godfather has someone special and a daughter. He's a good man, that's his reward. Mommy always used to say that... But I can't dwell on sadness, so we hop on the merry-go-round in the park and later grab a bite at a café. I chatter about school, and Uncle Seryozha seems genuinely interested.

"Why are you interested when Mommy and Daddy aren't?" I ask him.

"They're very busy," my godfather replies with a wry smile. "Everything will be all right, Button, you'll see!"

"I believe," I assure him, because I truly do. "Will you stay long?"

As it turns out, Uncle Seryozha will be with us until my birthday, which is just around the corner, and then he'll head back home. I didn't even notice how time flew by; it feels like New Year's Eve was just yesterday, and now my birthday is only a week away! I wonder why aunt Taisia doesn't visit us very often. I inquire with Uncle Seryozha, and he promises to find out.

My godfather also brought two large boxes, beautifully wrapped with ribbons, but he won't let me peek inside. I'm itching with curiosity! It doesn't seem fair! But Uncle Seryozha insists that everything is fair and flashes a smile. And I smile too, because he's my godfather! And I believe that everything will work out. Mommy and Daddy will reflect in their corner, and everything will fall into place. I believe it!

My birthday arrives unexpectedly, but I'm eagerly anticipating it, of course. It's the day when Mommy and Daddy are both home. They love me dearly, and I love them too. And pa... Uncle Seryozha is here as well. That's why the morning kicks off with my excited squeals as Daddy throws me up in the air, praising what a good girl I am! I'm turning eight years old today!

This day is solely mine, as Mommy and Daddy say. They don't argue on this day, and if anyone starts to bicker, Uncle Seryozha gives them a stern look, and everyone straightens up. Soon we'll be heading off for a holiday by the sea, just like last year, because that's the tradition. I'm quickly showered with presents, and I uncover what was in the two boxes Uncle Seryozha brought. A big bear, incredibly soft, and a whole lot of school supplies—five different sets of pencils, pens, crayons, and some other stuff I don't immediately recognize. Then we have a grand breakfast, a real feast!

Next stop: the circus! Followed by a trip to the cinema! And then onto the merry-go-rounds, but first, the circus! I'm bursting with excitement, bouncing up and down, but of course, we must eat first because food is very important. Breakfast is scrumptious, lovingly made by Mommy, well, for everyone, but especially for me. Then I slip into my new dress to look extra pretty. It's a light green dress adorned with beautiful multicolored butterflies that shimmer in the sunlight. I instantly fall in love with it—it's just so gorgeous!

We hop into the car and head to the circus, where there's a bustling crowd, especially of children, because the circus is for kids. We settle into our seats in the middle of the row, surrounded by others, and I eagerly await the show. I've been to the circus before, so it's nothing new to me—a circular arena, stairs, and inside... it's like a deep well, but we're in the third row, so it feels like everything will happen right before our eyes.

First come the clowns, entertaining us with their antics, pretending to run and tumble, and then the real show begins... Gymnasts, acrobats, juggling bottles high up, walking through the air, and even flying. It's all so mesmerizing! I applaud enthusiastically because it's just fantastic! Then come the animals, and even the tigers behave as gently as kittens. And the clowns continue to make me burst into laughter with their antics!

After the circus, I stroll around with a balloon on a string, sharing my excitement, as Uncle Seryozha calls it. I'm so full of joy that I refuse to notice if Daddy and Mommy aren't as cheerful as they usually are on my beloved birthday. I just don't want to! So, off we go to the park, where there are water shows, carousels, and more. Today, I'm determined to have as much fun as possible, as if something bad might happen if I don't. Later, I even confide in my little sister that I felt a bit scared earlier when I saw the way Mommy looked at Daddy during some interaction with another lady. But my little sister reassures me that it's normal for grown-ups to have such moments, and I realize that I just misinterpreted the situation, which is why I got scared.

And then, after my birthday... Well, initially, of course, the next day, I shared candy with everyone in my class, and they all wished me well too. And then the days rolled on, and Uncle Seryozha flew away, but Mommy and Daddy weren't as tense anymore, especially Daddy—he stopped arguing with Mommy, or at least I didn't hear them argue anymore. Mommy also seemed more at ease, and everything started feeling like it used to. I really, really want to believe that.

I end the year with straight A's, isn't that wonderful? Mommy is thrilled, and so is Daddy. They treat me to a big serving of ice cream to celebrate, but they remind me to eat it slowly so I don't get sick, because falling ill before the holiday would be a shame. The sea is waiting for us! It's waiting!

Daddy mentions again that we'll be driving there because there are no train tickets available. I ask him what that means. Apparently, it's possible that all the seats are already booked in advance, but it seems a bit odd to me, because Daddy had talked about taking the car a while ago. But maybe everyone just really wants to go to the sea? It should be interesting traveling by car, although it might get a bit boring since you have to sit for a long time and your bottom gets tired. But at least I can nap, especially with my little sister. I'll gaze out of the window a bit, also with my little sister, because it's intriguing! And then, when my classmates ask me how I spent my summer, I'll have plenty to tell them about.

In my dream, we have a room where my little sister lives, so we can play there. It's kind of boring, but I'm not upset because Daddy lets me take any toys with me. I pack so much stuff that it barely fits in the car, which makes Mommy grumble, or at least I think she's grumbling.

Finally, the day of departure comes. I'm settled in the car, but it's still very early and I'm still sleepy. So I go to my little sister's and Daddy heads to the sea. Mommy seemed to fall asleep when I left for my little sister's. There, we play for a bit, and then I suggest adding a shower to the room, and we start imagining it because my sister says bathrooms are better. We're having so much fun that I don't notice the time passing. Mommy wakes me up to feed me, and while she's feeding me, I see Daddy drinking from some green bottle. Later, Daddy starts smiling as if something fun was in that bottle.

"Have you been drinking?" Mommy asks in the car, sniffing.

"No, come on, honey, I'm driving," Daddy replies cheerfully, but I can hear the insincerity in his voice.

Is Daddy cheating on Mommy? Why would he do that?

I'm troubled by this question as we continue driving. Unable to sleep because of this question, I think of my little sister, wishing she could see the beautiful road too. We climb a hill, from where we can see something that looks like a strip of sea. I'm already excited to dive into the water, so I sit quietly to avoid getting in the way.

"Are you sure you haven't been drinking?" Mommy wonders again. Then I wonder: What if she had a premonition? "Answer me quickly!"

"Honey, let's not fight in the car!" Daddy replies with pressure, speeding up the car for some reason, but looking at Mommy.

"Stop it now!" Mommy almost screams, and then something happens.

I see something big and black coming towards the car, something is cracking, breaking, Mommy is screaming, and suddenly, I feel very painful and somehow hot. It hurts so much that I find myself in my little sister's arms all of a sudden. She tries to calm me down, but I'm shaking with fear. When I tell her about Daddy drinking from a bottle, my little sister sobs and holds me close.

"Why don't you sit here and play, and I'll take your place?" My little sister suggests it. "If it hurts or scares you, I've been through worse, but it's not good for you. As soon as everything is fine, we'll switch back!"

I wonder... My sister wants to protect me from pain or sadness. It's not really fair, but it's what she wants. While she's there, I'll play and sit in my room. It's familiar, so it won't be scary. I'll see if I can fall asleep. I agree, and my older sister takes me in her arms, leads me to the cot, and strokes me. She promises that I'll stay there until I'm no longer scared, so I just nod. And I kiss her goodbye because my sister is a hero.

A STROKE OF FATE

ELDER

My little one, Mashenka, has brought me more warmth and joy in one year than I've experienced in my entire life. It's a relief that she agreed to switch places because her parents are, to put it mildly, awful. One was drinking while driving, and the other was distracting him. What intelligence! Uncle Seryozha calls them nominees for the Darwin Award. They're probably just corpses by now, but I'm still trying to understand how badly the child was hurt. Now, I'll have a chance to find out.

I have no clue what's going on with our dreams, but for now, I'll put little Mashenka to bed and sit with her to comfort her. I have to face the pain now; there's no other way... Adults are such jerks! They had such a wonderful daughter, such a miraculous family, and they ruined it all. I don't understand why! What did that dyed fool want? What about that idiot who drank while driving? And now, Mashenka is left all alone! If anything happens to her, all the acquaintances and friends will vanish, and I don't know anyone. And if that happens, she'll end up in an orphanage, which she doesn't deserve. She's better off staying pure and bright. For those monsters, she has me. My whole life, they're monsters...

I wake up, tossing and turning, overwhelmed by pain. The siren blares familiarly from above, urging me to hold on, but it's hard to stay afloat, so I retreat back to my little sister. The pain is most intense in my legs, given the agony and the pleas; nothing seems right. Nor could it be.

"You're back already?" the little girl smiles at me. "It's only been less than a minute!"

"We're in the ambulance," I explain to her. "It's boring, so I'll sit with you. Can we play a game?"

"Sure!" My little sister's smile widens.

We start playing because right now, I need to distract her from her thoughts. She shouldn't dwell on what happened; she shouldn't. She taught me... no, she didn't teach me, she showed me how things can be different. Even though my father was about to betray her, and my mother's boyfriend turned out to be unlike her, she really showed me how things can be different. And now that the worst has happened, I desperately don't want her to leave. If she's crippled, there's only horror and nightmares ahead because nobody wants a disabled person in our world; I know that myself.

I try to wake up a couple of times while we're playing, but I realize I can't. So, I have to wait; I don't know what's happening there... Although, what am I thinking? It's clear what's happening – they're operating on the child. So, we have a chance not to be left disabled. A small chance, of course, because I don't believe in miracles; I'm not the optimistic type.

"It's my fault," she suddenly says to me. "I should have told Mommy that Daddy drank from that bottle."

"It's not your fault," I shake my head. "Your mom and dad are adults, and you're a child. They make their own decisions."

"What's going to happen now?" she asks softly.

"You're going to stay here now," I tell her gently. "I'll be here for you, and when things get better, you'll come back. That way, you won't cry and hurt your heart."

"What about you?" Mashenka asks softly.

"I've gotten used to a lot of things, my dear," I hug her, stroking her head as she likes.

"You're a real hero... heroine," she corrects herself. "Thank you!" And with that, we part ways for now. I wake up in reality, trying to grasp my surroundings. White sheets, the steady hum of machines, and the rhythmic beeping of a heart monitor. It's the ICU. My legs ache considerably, but it's bearable. Breathing is labored, but not suffocating. My ribs must have taken a hit too. But only time will heal them. But my legs... What's wrong with my legs? I attempt to move them, but the pain intensifies, prompting me to sob loudly. I forgot that my body was that of a child, never subjected to such trauma before.

"Are you awake?" I hear a gentle voice.

After a moment, a kindly face appears above me. It's a woman in a green uniform, offering me a drink, confirming she's a nurse. So I'm being cared for, which is reassuring. If not, it would be unsettling. In this unfamiliar body, there's hope for proper treatment.

"It hurts," I tell her. "Where's Mommy?"

"The doctor will be here shortly," she responds softly. "He'll explain everything. Just be patient, okay?"

Her tone betrays concern. It seems both my parents are seriously injured, and I'm alone. Grandfather isn't fond of Mashenka, so if he takes her, it's not out of kindness. And our godparents... we know nothing about them, not even their whereabouts. And the grim reality dawns on me - we're not at home, not in our hometown. We're in a resort or nearby. No one will send us "home," so it's likely an orphanage awaits us. Mashenka shouldn't have to endure that. Here comes the doctor.

"And here we have Masha, a miraculous survivor," the nurse announces, to which the doctor, an older man with gray hair and glasses, nods. He wears a matching suit, and that's all I can see for now.

"How is Masha doing?" someone asks.

"Road traffic accident, shattered legs, broken rib," my doctor explains briefly, likely to the attending physician. "High amputation of both legs, about... That's it. Rib is operated on, so...."

"No relatives?" the voice inquires.

"We're searching," the doctor responds succinctly. "Our police are on it. We'll find out soon enough."

It's clear to me. While the term "amputation" is vaguely familiar, from the context, I gather my legs are gone. Once again, I'm at the mercy of fate, and life's pleasures seem distant. Yet, there's a glimmer of hope, as in my past life. But we have to survive until December, and it's only August now. Will anyone remember Mashenka?

I doubt anyone would take a risk to claim me, or that anyone would feel pity for a child. People tend to forget good deeds, so there's little hope for kindness. Nonetheless, I provide my surname, home address, details about my grandfather and godparents. The doctor takes notes, promising to relay the information. But I doubt anyone will respond. Unless Uncle Serezha could help, but I know nothing about him except his name and that he lives in Germany. Finding him seems impossible, and it's unlikely he'll come to our aid...

How do I break the news to this little miracle that Mommy and Daddy won't be here anymore? How? Where do I find the words? How do I explain that she won't be able to run and play anymore, but will be confined to a wheelchair, surrounded by cruel people? I don't know how to say it, so I just cry. I cry and hold the little girl, left alone in the world, just like I once was.

"Mummy and Daddy..." she realizes, starting to cry with me.

"They... They..." I struggle to speak through my tears.

The doctors want to keep me asleep to help me cope with the wreckage of a lifetime, they say, so I spend a lot of time with Mashenka. She's incredibly smart, a true miracle, orphaned by the foolishness of the adults around her. My little sister, I'll never let anyone harm you, no way!

"You were right," Mashenka says, crying. "I'd rather stay here, if... if it's okay."

"You have to, little one," I hold her close, gently rocking her.

I think I've found my purpose. To protect this miracle from human cruelty, from harm... My little one understands everything, and she clings to me, and together we can face anything. I've made up my mind. We have to survive for six months. I'll make it through, I've been through worse.

When I wake up, the procedures start - doctors check my healing, do whatever they do, and then something happens that would have devastated the little girl, but I expected this kind of reaction from people, so I'm not surprised. Grandpa walks into the room. He looks at me with a familiar expression, one I've seen before in a past life, really, but I know that expression...

"No, you're mistaken," Grandpa says, grinning at me. "I don't know that girl."

"You're despicable," sighs the nurse, realizing what's happening.

"I'll get you!" shouts a stranger at me.

But they take him away, and from the screams I hear, they call the police. But I don't care, because the old man showed me exactly what I expected. And the nurse, aunt Taisia, sits beside me and just hugs me. And I cry, of course, because my body reacts naturally. But it would have devastated the little girl, because I'll never understand such betrayal. I was a terrible person, truly awful, and I deserved my fate, but Mashenka didn't deserve any of this!

Aunt Taisia is probably gone for good, but I expected that. It's foolish to hope that Uncle Seryozha will be found before December. In this world, money decides everything, as Vaskin's father taught me, so most likely, the old man will just sell the flat and get rid of everything, including Mashenka. I wonder if anything is left of her backpack. I'll have to ask later, but for now, I need to figure out where I'm going.

"What's going to happen to me?" I ask the nurse.

"You'll go to a children's shelter," she sighs. "An orphanage for..."

"A cripple," I finish harshly. "I've been abandoned, haven't I?"

"Whoever they find," she replies vaguely. "But they've arranged for a good children's shelter for you, so you won't be completely alone."

I don't know who paid for it, and honestly, I'm not eager to find out. There's a nod from me, and the nurse shares that back home, there was a TV ad, but there were no responses. However, some important person called in and covered the expenses for a "good" children's shelter. I'm not sure what that entails, as I've never been in such a situation before, but I have no choice but to wait and see where life leads me next. In the meantime, I'm receiving treatment, also covered, along with a specialized wheelchair, surprisingly not the cheapest one. It piques my interest when I hear about it, but my aunt is unaware of the benefactor's identity, so my curiosity remains unsatisfied.

Nearly a month later, I receive an answer to my question. I'll be discharged soon, causing a familiar anxiety to surface, though I'm as composed as my medication allows. Then, one afternoon, the man whom Mashenka referred to as the "scary black sorcerer" enters the ward. I'm not afraid of him, but he approaches me, crouches down, and gazes sadly into my eyes.

"Hello, little girl," he says somberly. "I'm the scary sorcerer, remember me?"

"I remember," I nod, attempting a joke. "Have you come to eat me?"

"No, little one," he shakes his head. "I've come to apologize. I can't take you in; I'm always on the move, so they won't allow it."

"I understand," I nod, realizing now who covered all my expenses.

I understand... and yet, I don't! Why would a stranger feel compelled to help me when my own grandfather, godmother, or even aunt Taisia, who must have seen the ad, didn't step in? What about my parents' friends and acquaintances? But then again, perhaps this uncle had genuine affection for Mashenka's mother. Only love could motivate such generosity toward a complete stranger. He shows me that not all people are selfish. Maybe that gives me a glimmer of hope for the future.

I'm discharged the following day. I've grown accustomed to the wheelchair, thanks to the "sorcerer's" intervention, which makes it much easier to navigate. But that's not all. Transportation from the children's shelter is arranged, along with Miss Vera, who will accompany me from now on. She'll offer support at the children's shelter and school, if needed. However, she's quick to clarify that she's not a mother. It's a relief that I'm in Mashenka's shoes; it would have been tough for her. As for me, I've never had a loving mother, so I nod in understanding.

"Keep your spirits up, little girl," the nurse tells me. "If I could, I would take you..."

That truly surprises me. A nurse willing to take...

someone like me? No pressure, just genuine care and warmth? I feel like I'm in a strange world. An uncle who owes me nothing contributes a substantial sum of money, and now a nurse is willing to offer her home? What's next? Perhaps this news leaves me off-kilter, so I tear up and hug her gratefully. Strangely enough, she seems to understand me. She shares her phone number, offering to keep in touch... It's a miraculous gesture, beyond comprehension.

Then Miss Vera arrives, signaling it's time for me to embark on my new journey.

ORPHANAGE

ELDER

THEY'RE TAKING me to another city. First, they wheeled me directly into a wheelchair and loaded me into a black minibus with tinted windows, securing me inside. Slowly, it pulled away from the hospital. This is where I encountered people. People who understand that a child needs at least some affection... There are no animals here... Let's see what happens next.

I didn't want to look out the window, so I leaned back and mentally went to my sister's room. She's probably waiting for me, though I've introduced her to the nurse and the "sorcerer." But did she grasp the situation? I'll find out now. It's crucial that Mashenka understands what happened, as it's a significant experience for her.

"Sis-ay-ay-ay!" cheers up the little one. "Tell me what happened, because I don't understand!"

That's exactly what I expected. I smile at her, sit down beside her, and start explaining what happened and why it's important. Sis listens intently, then shakes her head as if she disagrees. Curious about her perspective, I stop talking, allowing her a few moments to think, and then...

"No, it wasn't like that!" my little one smiles. "Listen, Mummy and Daddy have gone to heaven, right?"

I nod, as it seems the simplest explanation to me, and it's easier for a little girl like me to accept.

"Okay," she continues. "They'll love each other there and make another Masha, because I agreed right away to be taken by the scary black sorcerer. But he probably got full quickly, so he didn't finish me off. Instead, he gave me money to grow and get bigger. Then he'll come and take me, I guess. Don't worry, I'm okay with it. The important thing is that Mummy and Daddy are happy sitting on a cloud."

Oh, my little one... How she explains things to herself in a way that can't be argued, yet she's willing to sacrifice herself just to make those two fools happy. I wonder if they're pleased with what they've created. Are they content knowing that a sweet innocent child is ready to die to bring them happiness? How could they do that to her? How?!

. . .

I gently stroke Mashenka, who has found her own way to understand things, and I can't help but wonder what lies ahead. I won't allow her to be exposed to that harsh world; I won't! Let her remain an innocent angel, especially considering her parents... Maybe I can manage it, and then Uncle Seryozha will protect the little angel? But to even try, I have to make it to December, and right now, it's only mid-September. It makes sense; healing takes time, and my heart isn't cooperating well, which is understandable.

I bid farewell to Masha, who's engrossed in playing with her doll. I open my eyes to a somewhat large cityscape around me, bigger than where I received treatment, definitely. It's no longer by the sea, but that's inconsequential now, as the sea holds little significance for me. But that's not the focus at the moment, as the minibus is granted entry through a gate, leading to my new... confinement. Let's be honest - with no say in the matter, cut off from the outside world, it feels like a prison, whatever you call it. And to subject a little girl accustomed to warmth and care to such a place? Absolutely not!

"We've arrived," Miss Vera informs me. "Now, we'll head up to the first floor, where you'll be staying. Your belongings have been moved there, and the orphanage will take care of the rest."

"Okay," I nod, realizing I have no say in the matter.

I'm carefully assisted out of the car, with the driver taking off until Monday. So, it's Saturday. That gives me two days to settle in, which is reassuring. I head to school, and though

Mashenka's memories don't include primary school material, somehow, I recall everything. It's like a gift from Santa Claus; at least I won't be behind.

I wonder if I'll face bullying? Though it's just second grade, perhaps not... And Vera assures she'll be there to assist, ensuring I can use the restroom in peace. Alright, where to next? A cheery-colored small house leaves me feeling melancholic; it's fortunate Mashenka isn't here to see it. I don't pay much attention, not interested just yet. Through the entrance, past the janitor's office, exchanging greetings with artificial smiles. A lift to my floor... One that I can reach myself. A short corridor with rubberized carpeting; it's obvious why... A plain wooden door to the right. A plaque with my name on it.

The door swings open, revealing a small hallway, an open bathroom door, a closet, a bed, two bedside tables, a TV, and a table. It's a well-furnished studio apartment, especially for an orphan. There's even a small kitchenette with a fridge and microwave. A surprisingly nice setup for someone abandoned by everyone except her mother's ex-lover. It's ironic... Out of all the friends, relatives, and close ones, only a complete stranger turned out to be humane....

Alright, let's see what unfolds. Miss Vera explains what's where. The belongings are just the ones Mashenka took to the sea; what happened to the rest isn't specified, but I already understand. Grandfather did what he could; there was no other way. Alright, the wrongs will be righted eventually, sooner or later karma catches up. If not in this life, then in the next; I truly believe that.

"Get used to it," Miss Vera instructs, showing me how to use the facilities. "If you need anything, there's a call button."

With that, she bids goodbye and leaves, leaving me alone in the room. I feel like spitting, but it's futile... How much does it take for an eight-year-old, ripped away from her world, stripped of everything familiar, to just accept being left alone? How would I react if I were younger? I can't even imagine... And yet, they just took it - "this is your box, from now on and forever."

I wheel myself to the window and gaze at the street. In the orphanage yard, kids play football right beside the prams, but I don't want to watch them; my eyes are fixed on the fence, where life carries on with cars passing by and people walking. I know that Mashenka and I are lucky to have found someone who provided us with money. It could have been much, much worse, because....

"If you cry, I'd probably cry all the time," my little sister says sadly. "It's good we switched, because at least I have legs here."

My little sister's words hit me hard. It dawns on her that our parents are gone, and she's left without her legs... Fate can be incredibly cruel. I wish I could bear all of Mashenka's pain for her and let her continue to enjoy a happy life, but I know it's impossible. As I ponder this, I hear something ringing in the distance, likely an alarm clock. After bidding goodbye to Mashenka, I reluctantly return to reality.

I rise from bed, maneuver into the wheelchair, and switch off the alarm clock. I have an hour before I need to leave, ample time to get ready. Dressing myself is a challenge; being an eight-year-old, I struggle to know how to dress appropriately for the weather. It's just another cruelty in a series of many. And Vera, she hardly grasps the extent of her own cruelty... People, even the good ones, can be quite callous creatures.

Heading to the kitchen, I opt for yogurt for breakfast, knowing there's school breakfast available. I hope it hasn't spoiled. Unlike my sister, I'm not accustomed to domestic tasks, but I manage to dress myself, concealing my prosthetic limbs. The sight of my artificial limbs, tinged blue-red, stirs up emotions, but I suppress them fiercely. There's no one here to witness my tears.

After brushing my teeth and washing my face, I dress, mindful of potential prying eyes. The question of how I'll manage using the toilet at school looms over me. There's a suitable toilet here, but what about there? Recalling the simplicity of my previous school's facilities, I choke back sobs. Despite being fourteen, I still yearn for affection and warmth —things I've never truly had, especially since Mashenka entered my life. But such wishes seem futile now.

I scolded myself and finally got dressed. I grabbed a

simple school bag with my textbooks and notebooks already packed and left the apartment. It's not locked here, so security is practically nonexistent. Today, I'm heading to second grade, although I already know everything we'll be learning. That means I don't have to focus solely on my studies; I can pay attention to what's happening around me. My hair got burned in the accident, so now I have a bob that covers my ears, making it harder for anyone to grab it.

As I step into the elevator, I press the green button. If I were fifteen, or even twelve, I might be able to explain everything, but at eight years old, I'm clueless. That's just the way it is. I need to brace myself because school can be a place of provocation, hatred, and the desire to hurt others, all learned from their parents. While I've seen a few exceptions, they're rare. So, I'm not expecting any miracles. Downstairs, Miss Vera is already waiting, checking her watch. Her smile lacks warmth, merely a formality.

"Are you ready?" the chaperone asks rhetorically. "Get in the car."

"Am I going alone?" I question, noticing the minibus's emptiness.

"I'm your company," Miss Vera confirms. "There was another girl, but she couldn't handle it. But you're holding up well, good for you."

I don't even want to know what she means by that. The other child could have faced serious consequences. As the older one, I understand better, but I feel remorse for my past actions, especially towards Karina. The minibus starts moving, and I contemplate our destination, likely the regional center. I'm unsure how schools for kids like me differ from regular ones, putting me in the same boat as Mashenka. Sighing, I inquire about safety precautions from the attendant, steering away from Mashenka's experience.

"Since you seem to understand, I'll be brief," she says softly. "No one can harm you during recess, in the restroom, or in the cafeteria as long as you're with me, but I won't be chasing after you, got it?"

"Thank you," I acknowledge, realizing I'm only vulnerable in the classroom. They won't physically harm me, but insults and attempts to provoke are expected. It's a game I'm familiar with, so I know what to expect and how to handle it. While I may be physically weaker, the chaperone will prevent any physical harm, and I need to avoid being baited. We'll manage.

The minibus halts in front of a squat three-story building. They help me out of the vehicle, and I accompany the escort, who walks with dignity. I notice the ramp nearby, so I won't need to crawl, which is a relief. I've learned not to trust people's kindness, especially those who work with children.

"Hey, hold on, where's your change!" A teenager, probably around fourteen, tries to confront me.

"Right where my feet are," I respond calmly, but he persists in trying to push me away.

"Stop it immediately!" Miss Vera's stern voice sends

shivers down my spine, even frightening the local guardian. It's a show of authority, and it works.

Inside, there are ramps instead of lifts, but since the primary school is on the ground floor, it's not an issue. Miss Vera doesn't take me directly to a classroom, which makes sense. First, we'll meet with the head teacher or the teacher, and then I'll be introduced to the class. As I glance around, I notice the dreary, gray corridors adorned with worn-out children's drawings, realizing that this place isn't exactly cheerful. However, it doesn't seem like a prison either; there are no strict supervisors or authoritarian figures lurking around.

Finally, we arrive at a door with the sign I anticipated. It's time to brace myself; they'll likely try to intimidate me and bring me to tears in this office. Well, I'm prepared. Are you, you bullies?

SCHOOL FOR DISABLED CHILDREN

ELDER

Recalling the unsettling gaze of the head teacher, I realize she's accustomed to seeing children scared and in tears. So when I didn't display the usual fear but arrived with an escort, she put on a show of being delighted to see me. However, I understand I must be cautious. Danger lurks everywhere, and I feel like a nobody, a forgotten eight-year-old nobody. It's fortunate that Mashenka isn't here to witness this.

Led into the classroom, Vera bids me farewell, quietly urging me not to be afraid. She understands the situation perfectly well, as anyone would. I hope she has some means to protect me. They won't harm me physically, but when I'm frightened... well, that can be exploited if need be.

God, how I wish I could be with Mashenka on a deserted island, away from people. I'm growing weary, too weary of this world too quickly, it seems. But I can't indulge in such thoughts because the classroom door swings open, revealing the class. It's a standard class, fifteen students, not all confined to wheelchairs, so there are also those with mental challenges.

As I'm introduced, it becomes evident that nobody is interested. One might find solace in that, but we're just eight years old! This can't be normal! Even at my age, I realize that eight-year-olds shouldn't be so apathetic. What's happened to them, and what awaits me? There's no answer to that question, but there's little choice. Lord, if you're there, help me make it until December!

I'm directed to a seat next to a girl who sits expressionless, much like Karina. It's as if she's shut off from the world. The thought of Mashenka ending up like that pains me, but I take a few deep breaths, and the feeling subsides. Apparently, my reaction doesn't go unnoticed as the teacher approaches me.

"Don't be frightened, Mashenka," she says softly. "All the children here... have lost their parents. Not all of them can cope. But you're doing great."

I nod, sensing genuine empathy in her words. It must be tough for her to be here among these silently suffering children. Looking around the classroom again, I realize I won't face bullying here. More than half of the kids seem emotionally detached. Why are they like this, and why isn't anyone helping them? It's a futile question, I know, but I can't help feeling sorry for them.

The lesson begins, and I notice the teacher's struggle to engage the students, but nobody responds except me. It's as if they're not even present. I feel sorry for the teacher, but mostly for myself, especially when recess arrives. The teacher sits beside me and begins to speak.

Miss Vera enters the classroom and observes the teacher discussing each of the motionless children. They hardly move or react to anything. How did they end up in this classroom? They must have been escorted here too. It's going to be challenging to study in this environment. It's nothing like what I initially thought; it feels like I'm surrounded by the emotionally numb. It's unsettling, facing fifteen Karinas... I don't know how to handle it. I just don't know.

"Do they have psychologists here, maybe even psychiatrists?" I inquire.

"They should," the teacher acknowledges, while Miss Vera lets out a sigh.

"You mean..." I pause, unable to voice my assumption, but Miss Vera voices what I already know.

"You're fortunate," she responds briefly. "You managed on your own."

"I get it," I affirm in return.

I comprehend everything clearly. If it weren't for me and all of it fell on Mashenka, no one would have bothered much - they'd have medicated her, labeling her as unstable, and that would be the end of it. Who cares about orphans? Especially if you lack money and a wealthy uncle to back you up. I grasp it completely because I'm not an eight-year-old child anymore, and I'm not sheltered. While I'm busy spinning tales for all the adults about what I lack, behind my back is a child, a true angel, whom I won't surrender to them.

Attempting to muster up some indignation, I no longer pay attention to my classmates but simply provide correct answers to the teacher, earning her smile. Later, Miss Vera, vigilant as ever, guides me to the cafeteria. She doesn't directly interfere but keeps a watchful eye on the students when needed, abruptly halting others and thus asserting my status. It's quite timely because I catch a couple of hostile glances.

At the serving line, Miss Vera doesn't intervene as I collect the tray, finding the school breakfast: bread, a pat of butter, and clumpy porridge. It's semolina, though no one seems to have any illusions... I don't either; this is a state institution, not my mother's kitchen. So the breakfast is reasonably adequate, and the lumps, I'll manage.

Suddenly, I feel oddly mature, despite inhabiting a child's body. Perhaps it's because I have a baby on my back. Yes, that must be the reason... Right.

The first day of school passes relatively smoothly, but it's during the ride home that I understand why my classmates all seem so withdrawn. They were merely lumped together, and it was assumed that I'd be in a similar state. Essentially, just to avoid complications, they were grouped together. Thus, they're all alike... Then, presumably, I'd be transferred to the livelier ones, but I doubt they'll do that, from what I can gather. It's more convenient for them, and nobody here considers the children.

I've never truly considered what it's like to be parentless... Carina, I apologize! I'm sorry! Tears stream down my face, but Miss Vera silently acknowledges my thoughts, and I cry because here, I fully grasp the weight of my actions. I understand, and it suddenly feels unbearably painful, sorrowful, so... I find myself enveloped in my sister's embrace, continuing to weep. And she holds me, stroking my head just as I did for her a little while ago.

"Is it really that terrible?" Mashenka asks me softly.

"Awful, but not like that," I shake my head. "It's just that I've come to realize what I've done...

"You've already paid for it, and you're not a bad person anymore," the little angel reassures me. "You're very good... If it weren't for you..."

And together, we weep... Nestled in a bed that isn't there, we hug each other and let out our tears.

Fortunately, I know how to avoid taking pills, so I discreetly dispose of the prescribed medication down the toilet. The doctors didn't even bother examining my heart; they simply prescribed drugs that make you feel lifeless. But I'm not naive; I understood their intentions. The attendant beside me is as cold as stone, a mere statue of indifference. If it weren't for

Mashenka, I might have crumbled under the weight of it all; it's just too much to bear.

Somehow, September passed by unnoticed, followed by October, and now November is looming. It's cold, damp, and rainy... My stumps ache with every movement, every shift in the weather, sometimes to the point of agony, but there's no one to vent to. I attempted once, but quickly realized it's futile.

"It seems like there's nothing for you to hurt," Miss Vera replies indifferently, almost bringing tears to my eyes, but I hold back.

I endure, dreaming of the day when I can confront her. Not to harm her physically, no, but to shatter her indifferent facade! What a bunch of grown-ups! Heartless! Cruel! Disgusting! I find myself crying again... Tears have become a frequent visitor, and December is still a whole month away. How will I survive this month?

There's no clear answer... In my room, I contemplate how to shield myself from the pain. It's fortunate that I'm somewhat grown-up; Mashenka would be inconsolable. She cries often, but at least she doesn't dwell on it, and I introduce her to the few good books and films I've encountered before I became bitter.

I don't know how, but it works! It seems you can freeze the moments for Mashenka, and time won't pass for her... She won't be utterly alone. Tonight, I'll try it out, and hopefully, it will soothe her. If successful, I might be able to spare her tears. If not, I'll give her tasks and educate her as if in school.

I'll do anything to keep that baby from crying... Our warmth is all we have. There's no external warmth at all, as if adults fail to realize how crucial it is for children. Or maybe they do understand, but they just want to reduce the number of us, especially the disabled? Can people truly be so heartless?

Could people really want to torment children? But if so... Then we must resist, at any cost, because I'll pay any price! Any price at all, as long as that baby lives! As long as she smiles, even if it's from her pram, but that genuine smile we once knew! I'll do whatever it takes...

Back at school, where they no longer target me - they're accustomed to the chaperone. The teacher is decent but exhausted, and I don't interact much with others, greeting every adult I encounter just in case. I don't want to find out how they might retaliate for disrespecting me, though children don't seem to be physically harmed here; I don't see any signs of it.

The lessons blur into a monotonous haze, as there's nothing new for me, and the classmates... Wait, where's the girl who sat beside me? And the other two boys? They've either been moved to another class or to a more apparent location. Something tells me it's the latter. I'll ask the teacher and see what she says, and more importantly, how to respond...

Over these past months, my faith in people has completely crumbled. Sometimes I even question if I was ever as cruel as this. Back then, I was fighting with girls my own age, who theoretically could fight back, like Carina. But this cruelty towards those who can't defend themselves is on another level entirely. It would almost be better to be physically hit than to endure this cold indifference. Well, that's just my perspective... I'm not an expert, so it's just how I see it...

School... It's survivable, I suppose. If you overlook the dullness of the classroom, the crowdedness, the constant feeling of threat, you can manage. And it's wise to be cautious with breakfast; a sandwich is preferable, considering the taste of the porridge... I'll refrain from elaborating on that.

"Where's my neighbor?" I asked. "Is she sick?"

"Yes," the teacher quickly seized on the question, avoiding eye contact. "Very sick indeed."

We all know that "sickness." It's called "death," or "mental institution," which probably doesn't make much difference to the girl. But I suspect she's deceased, especially since the teacher's obviously lying. Why lie? To "avoid alarming" us? Or was she explicitly instructed to lie? I don't know... After what I've been through, I see a conspiracy in everything. Regardless, my suspicions are confirmed by the teacher's falsehood. Mashenka's fate is likely the same - death from boredom. But these schemers underestimated Mashenka; she's shielded from them, and instead, I'm here. I used to be one of them, so I can see through their tricks.

The school day passes swiftly; the tests are ridiculously easy, but I understand why. If their goal is to eliminate as many children as possible, there's no point in educating them. It makes sense to me. So far, everything I've observed supports that theory. I wonder if they'll push them to the limit or just wait it out. And as for me, what's their plan?

We'll have to wait and see how they attempt it, though there's only faint hope. I doubt there are any humans left among these beings. I simply don't believe it.

At the end of the lesson, my suspicions are further confirmed. Our teacher, who had been playing nice all this time, approaches me with feigned concern in her voice.

"Do you miss your parents a lot?" she asks, with fake sadness.

"Not at all," I respond, smiling to conceal my disdain. "I don't remember them at all."

The flash of anger in my eyes confirms what I've just heard. They're all just animals, God! Okay, I may have been bad, but what did the little ones do to deserve this? What have they done to them?!

DED MOROZ AND THE CHANCE

ELDER

AND THEN IT HIT ME: if I succeed, the baby will be all alone! So, I need to teach her how to take care of herself. She'll be looked after, but she needs to learn too, who knows? I don't pity myself at all; this little girl has become everything to me. She's probably the reason for my existence, so doing whatever it takes is easy for me. As long as she lives, as long as she smiles, as long as she's happy.

"Look, this is how you change seats," I show her. "It wouldn't be fair if only I knew how to do it, right?"

"Yes! I want to learn too!" Masha enthusiastically joins in. "What's the right way to do it?"

We switch places, and I teach her everything I already know. I really need to get her ready... But I don't know how to prepare her for when I won't be around. Maybe Uncle

Seryozha can look after her. Yes, I'm considering asking Santa Claus to swap me for... Well, to pay me so the little girl can find a family. I really hope I can make it happen because if not, we won't stand a chance against those things—they'll find a way to get us sooner or later.

It's crucial to me that the baby can live and smile. It's crucial because I don't see any other options. So, I'm getting her ready, and I'm slowly making her realize that one day I might not be here. Mashenka seems to like what we're doing so far, but I'm hesitant to say it outright. It's cowardly, I know, but it's better this way... It's really tough for me, it's just incredibly tough. And it's not easy for her either because no one has hugged us in months, and I want to hug her so much that tears well up in my eyes.

I let out a heavy sigh. Even though I've managed to freeze time, Mashenka is gradually growing sadder, and I can see why. Anyone would understand why, so it's not surprising. That's why I know we don't have much time because sooner or later, Mashenka will want to leave. She's an angel, a very delicate being, not suited for our world at all. God willing, Uncle Seryozha turns out to be a good person, and my sacrifice won't be in vain. Because if he doesn't take the baby...

Maybe I shouldn't be doing this. What if the godfather turns out to be just like those creatures? Then this exchange would be pointless... Completely pointless! It's a shame I hardly believe in God... I don't even have anyone to pray to, let alone ask. My ray of sunshine is confident that my godfather won't abandon me, but am I confident? I don't know.

One day, the chaperone tells me we're going to a Christmas tree in the city. Could it be that the Santa Claus at the tree is real? Not an actor, but the one who offered me the choice? Well, considering some magic, I guess it's possible. So, I quickly get dressed, having already made sure my feet are warm, and in a few minutes, I'm ready.

"Let's go," Miss Vera nodded, and I silently prayed for Ded Moroz to be real. Not for myself, but for my dearest sister!

As the minibus started moving, I couldn't find a seat. My sister's life depended on it working out. She's the only one who truly matters to me, the reason I exist... I kept calling out to Ded Moroz with all my might. My sister deserves all the luck! She hasn't harmed anyone! Please!

When we stopped in the car park, the driver looked into my eyes and sighed. He assisted me onto my wheelchair, and then I propelled myself forward. I sensed he wanted to hug me, but perhaps it wasn't allowed. We reached the tree, and my heart sank - it was just an actor. The real Ded Moroz was our only hope, but I couldn't see any options. Then, everything changed. Instead of the actor, he appeared, with the Snow Maiden beside him... Did I succeed?

"You called for me, Masha," Ded Moroz said. "What's wrong? Do you want your legs back?"

"I want to ask..." I replied quietly, gathering my courage.

"Ask, child," he nodded, smiling.

"Is it possible to find Mashenka's godfather?" I asked, tears welling up. "She'll perish in this cold."

"We can," Ded Moroz replied. "But everything comes at a cost. What are you willing to do?"

"Anything!" I declared, meeting his gaze with confidence. "Just let me bid farewell to my little sister!"

"Goodbye," he nodded, embracing me. "See, my granddaughter? She's redeemed herself and now she's sacrificing herself..."

"But Grandpa!" I heard before embracing Masha.

Now comes the hardest part - telling Mashenka what I've done and that I won't be here anymore, but my godfather will. As I explain, she understands everything and breaks down, clinging to me desperately. Her tears are heart-wrenching, and I can't help but cry with her. Then, we both feel the embrace of Ded Moroz and the Snow Maiden, as if in real life. It's the first hug we've had in months, and it brings forth even more tears.

"I can't guarantee your complete safety," he says, somewhat unclearly. "But I'll offer you a chance. Once the older Masha pays her dues, I'll manipulate time and space. The younger one will learn how to rescue the older, but whether she does so depends on her and her partner. Consider it a test for all of you."

"And the reward if they survive?" the Snow Maiden inquires, but her grandfather only offers a smile. With New

Year's Eve approaching, it's evident that it will remain a mystery.

"I'll save my little sister! I promise!" the younger one exclaims, unwilling to be separated from me, but our opinion isn't sought.

"It's time," Ded Moroz decides, and everything shifts.

It feels like I'm watching the scene from afar. Ded Moroz transforms once more, holding Masha, who appears bewildered and on the verge of tears. Miss Vera observes with curiosity but refrains from intervening. My little sister finally comprehends the situation and begins to cry, but she's not allowed to shed tears.

"Hey, sir!" Ded Moroz calls out to someone. "Have you lost someone?"

Miss Vera noticeably twitches, and the person summoned swiftly turns towards the performer and spots Mashenka. I recognize him - it's Uncle Seryozha. He stares for what seems like a minute, then rushes over, moving so fast it's almost as if he teleported to Ded Moroz.

"Masha! Masha! You're alive!" he exclaims, nearly snatching the child from the performer's arms, cradling her gently as my youngest sibling squeals with delight.

YOUNGER

Sis! She... She... She... She... She saved me all this time! She shielded me, hid her tears from me, and now she's here for me! For me... I cling to her, refusing to be separated, but the Snow Maiden explains that Santa Claus has altered time and space so my little sister can be rescued. Then I spot Papa Seryozha! I cry out with both joy and pain.

"Mashenka! My little one! Alive!" He's nearly in tears, hugging me gently as only a father could.

"Daddy! Daddy, save her! Save her! Save her!" I sob, knowing my little sister is dying in the snow somewhere.

"Leave the child be," Miss Vera tries to approach, but a stranger stops her, and Papa Seryozha's expression turns serious.

"Who needs saving, little one?" He asks calmly.

"My little sister! Save her! They took her into the woods! In the snow! Save her!" I shout, surrounded by a crowd.

I should be relieved that Papa Seryozha is here, but my mind is only on my little sister. Daddy pulls out his phone, calling someone, surrounded by police officers listening intently.

"Do you know where she is?" Papa Seryozha asks me. "Sashka!" He calls to someone. "Coordinate with the locals!"

"Alright," nods the man speaking to Miss Vera. "Carry on."

"We've been searching for you, little one," my uncle... Papa Seryozha says. "The police and I couldn't find you... But what about my little sister? Where is she?"

"She saved me all this time," I whimper. "If it wasn't for her... And they took her away... Save me, Daddy!"

A big car stops nearby, and Papa Seryozha jumps in with me in his arms, forgetting the stroller, but I don't care. Everything feels like a dream where I can save my little sister, so I guide Papa Seryozha on how to find her. The car roars to life, sirens blaring behind us. Papa Seryozha tells me I've been missing for three months, even with the police searching. He's relieved to have found me, assuring me that my legs don't matter, because I'm still loved. And I cry, feeling his embrace after so long.

The car speeds off, trees flashing by outside. Papa Seryozha likely wants to reach my little sister as quickly as possible. I'm terrified she'll die! As we drive, I tell Daddy... Well, Uncle Seryozha, who's my godfather now that my real parents are in heaven. And he agrees to be my daddy! He says it himself! So I recount my little sister's story, how hard it was, and how she shielded me so I wouldn't cry.

"Your girl seems to mean everything to you," some uncle remarks. "But perhaps a bit too much..."

"That makes sense," Daddy nods, pulling me close and gently stroking me. "How have you been, little one?" he asks affectionately.

"If it weren't for my sister, I would have died," I answer him honestly. "So, only Mommy and Daddy went to heaven to create another Masha there, because I was attacked by a terrible black sorcerer who only bit my legs..."

"Jesus," the uncle murmurs softly. "Poor children..."

"Did your little sister have an accident too?" Daddy inquires.

"No, Dad, she used to be mean, but not anymore. Something in her back broke, and she can't walk," I start my story, feeling slightly calmer. "But some evil uncle wants to harm her, and right now..."

I start crying again, and my dad makes a phone call for assistance. I didn't realize he was so important, that the police listened to him, and that there were people here... But it's reassuring. We'll find my little sister, and we'll be together again. Even if they harm her, I would do anything for her. I talk about orphanage, about the pills people take there, and how my little sister knows not to take them.

"Bless her heart," the same uncle hums, shaking his head.

"Yeah, Button wouldn't have made it," Daddy agrees, stroking my head as I reach for his hand. "The monsters around here... It's okay, baby, it's over."

At that moment, the car stops. Daddy jumps out, lifting me in his arms, and a police officer rushes to him. Daddy gestures in a certain direction and says there's a child freezing in the forest, and we need to find him. He receives a solemn nod, and in a few minutes, we're all racing toward the forest, where I sense my little sister lies.

I reach out for her with all my might, and Daddy holds me tightly so I don't fall. He doesn't seem surprised about my missing legs, but all I want now is to embrace my little sister, nothing else! To hold her, to feel her, to hear her voice again, because she's saved me so many times! She saved me from death, from sorrow, from everything...

So, we were running, and then Daddy handed me to someone else, rushing to the girl lying still in the snow. It's my little sister, I can see her! I can feel her! I reach out for her with all my strength, but...

"Be patient, little one," the man holding me says. "Your daddy is going to save your little sister."

He says it with such confidence that I believe him. I just trust that Daddy will fix everything. Because he's Daddy! And she's my sister! She'll make it through because she's so good!

"Get a stretcher," Daddy says calmly. "Put it in my car just like that, and we'll sort it out."

"We'll stay here," the policeman tells us. "Since you're saying it's attempted murder..."

"Great," Papa Seryozha nods. "Then let's hurry. The child has hypothermia, and the younger one needs to be checked over. I don't like something..."

"What's there to like," the policeman sighs.

Once in the car, I collapse onto my little sister, calling out to her and stroking her, and she just puts her arm around me. And she calls me by my name. In that moment, I try to understand what's happening, but I can't, because I fall asleep. It's like the lights went out.

SALVATION

ELDER

That's it... The younger has found a family, someone to care for her, hug her, and comfort her. I've done all I could, and now I'm ready to accept my fate. Some might say I've repented for what I did, but that's not the main thing. The main thing is that Mashenka will smile. The main thing is that she'll have someone to keep her warm, because Uncle Seryozha won't abandon her. He held her so close, closer than anyone ever held me...

I wonder if Christians are right about hell, which I probably deserve. Hot frying pans, boiling tar... Let it be. I'll be warmed by memories of my baby girl's smile, the touch of her hands. However painful it may be, I can handle it because I had my baby girl.

"You've redeemed yourself," Santa's voice reaches me. - "And now we'll see what we can do for you."

"The important thing is that the baby will be happy," I whisper faintly, feeling myself fading in the snow.

At first, I feared it was Mashenka's body, but I realized it was my own exhausted fourteen-year-old body. I lay face down in the snow, too weak to fight and slowly freezing. Perhaps I should just fall asleep, that's all. I remember reading that freezing people simply drift off to sleep, and death comes quietly, without pain.

From afar, the wind carries the sound of a siren, and the flicker of hope inside me dies. No one needs me here, not at all, and no one will find me. I close my eyes, mentally bidding farewell to Mashenka, who has given me more warmth and affection than I've ever known in my short, pointless life. May she find happiness!

But as if in response to my thoughts, I hear footsteps running. I hear the snow crunching and a baby crying. Must be a hallucination, they said you hallucinate before you die in the hospital, I recall. Good hallucinations... Before you die, feeling saved. It makes me smile, but the cold grows stronger, reminding me that Death is drawing nearer.

Something falls beside me, hands turn me over, and through the mist of tears, I see someone who can't possibly be here. Uncle Seryozha quickly examines me. I feel his touch, and involuntarily, I reach out to him. But how? How did he get here? After all, I'm not a little girl. How did he know? At that moment, I believe in miracles.

They lift me and carry me somewhere, laying me down very gently, as if someone needs me, as if I were the youngest. Maybe they just made a mistake, but then I realize - no, they didn't. A literal baby falls on top of me, calling me, rubbing me, and I just can't believe it.

"Baby, Masha, don't cry, it's not good for you," I try to say, but at that very moment the light goes out. Everything disappears, and I find myself in the baby's room. She runs up and hugs me, crying.

"Sis, my darling, my love," the little girl who immediately ran up to me, because she has legs here, "we found you! We found you! Daddy will save you!"

"But how? We're at different times..." I say, though I'm not sure about that anymore.

"The Snow Maiden told me!" Masha proudly answers me. "She told me how to find you, and that time had changed, and Popochka saved you, and there were lots of police, and someone else, but I was only thinking about you...."

"My little one..." I hold her close to me. "My little sunshine."

I don't think about how it is that we are in a shared dream again, all that matters to me is that she is warm. That's all that matters... Oh, we must have fallen asleep at the same time, it will scare people, we have to go back! I push my little sister, who understands everything, and come out myself, immediately finding myself in the bed of the ICU room, which I know very well. Where's my little sister?

"Don't panic," said the concerned voice of Uncle Seryozha. "Your little sister is near, turn your head and you'll see."

"Thank you... - oops, echoes.....

After a moment I realise that it's not an echo, it's Mashenka. I need to persuade her not to fidget or get nervous, but Uncle Seryozha understands everything himself - he just moves our beds apart and puts Mashenka's hand on mine, telling us both not to worry.

"All the bad things are over for both of you," he says confidently, and then asks someone: "Well, what about you?

"The younger one has a high amputation, but there are questions," a bassy and velvety voice answers him. "But with the older one... There are traces of psychoactive substances in her blood and hair, so there are questions about her aggressiveness, and depression, too. Forensics is working on it.

"What local authorities?" Uncle Seryozha asks, to which he is handed a paper.

I see a hand appear out of thin air with a white sheet of paper in it. I realize that it is some kind of paper, and looking at it, Uncle Seryozha starts to smile. So it's good news. And I lie there and can't understand what really happened, despite the explanations of the younger one, and, most importantly, what will happen next. To live in our country like me... I already know what it is, and I'd rather die, honestly.

"What will happen to me?" I whispered softly, hoping she wouldn't hear me.

I felt like a stranger in his eyes, knowing I wouldn't be needed, but I needed to ask for the sake of the younger one's understanding. Uncle Seryozha grasped not only the question but also its underlying meaning. He sighed heavily, repositioned the bed, fetched a chair, and settled between us, placing his warm hand on mine.

"The little one suddenly found herself all alone," Uncle Seryozha said calmly. "We'll figure out why later. But she had no one and nothing, and at that time, you were there for her, protecting her, offering hope. Isn't that right?"

"Yes, Daddy!" the little girl responded. "If it weren't for my big sister..."

"You're wondering what will happen," he continued, gently stroking both of us. "You, like her, will have a mommy, a daddy, and a big sister if you choose to join us. You'll live in a home filled with love, warmth, and trust. Not here, I'll take you to Germany, where our story will be very different."

"And how do they feel about... special girls?" I struggled to articulate the words.

"To the special girls," Uncle Seryozha smiled. "We call them that because they're very special. What do you say, my dear?" he asked affectionately. "Will you come with us?"

"Yes..." I whispered, fighting back tears. "Papa Seryozha..."

YOUNGER

When I open my eyes, I recognize the hospital room. I've been in one like this many times before, so I'm not scared. But where is my little sister? Daddy, whom I spot immediately, reassures me that Sis is nearby and helps me feel her presence. Despite feeling weak, I'm not afraid because Daddy is here, and he won't leave me.

I haven't forgotten about my parents who passed away and went to heaven. They'll have another Mashenka there, so I don't have them anymore. But now I have Daddy Seryozha, and maybe more than just him? How does his beloved feel about me? Am I a stranger to her? I'm not sure.

"Daddy says calmly, "The little one suddenly found herself all alone. We'll figure out why later. But she had no one and nothing, and at that time, you were there for her, protecting her, offering hope. Didn't you?"

"Yes, Daddy!" I shout, because if it weren't for her... And I want to say more, but somehow I can't. "If it weren't for my little sister."

"You're wondering what will happen," he continues, stroking me gently. "You'll have a mommy, a daddy, and a big sister, just like Button, if you accept us. You'll live in a home where you'll be loved, cared for, and never betrayed. Not here, I'll take you to Germany, where we'll have a very different storybook ending."

"I'm... we're getting a mommy?" I ask in surprise, and Daddy smiles.

"Yes, and mommy and big sister will be there," he nods, and then little sister starts to cry, and I understand why.

"Why are you so important?" I ask. "Everyone listens to you!"

"We searched for you so hard, Button," he answers, embracing his crying little sister. "No one wanted to say anything, and your grandfather..."

"I know," I nod knowingly. "He said he didn't know me, just like he said..."

"My baby!" Daddy hugs me with his other arm, and then, after a moment's silence, he continues. "We found the hospital where... where you were, we found out that you were there, but we couldn't find out more."

"I was at children's shelter," I explain. "A scary black sorcerer paid for me, and I was there. It was peaceful, but very cold. If it weren't for my sister..."

"Not everything is straightforward with that children's shelter," Daddy sighs. "But I have a lot of friends, and we got the German special authorities involved, so they helped me."

Realizing I need to ask my little sister about what Daddy is talking about, not because I don't trust him, but because she knows everything, I snuggle up to Daddy, feeling safe and unafraid. Then, a man quietly enters the room, handing something to Daddy, who releases us both to take it, examining it under the light.

"So, the surgery had these effects," Daddy reflects. "Well, we'll assess it back home... Will they be fine for the airplane?"

"They'll manage," the unfamiliar man asserts confidently. "Their conditions are dire, as you can see, and we're on our own."

"I understand," Daddy acknowledges with a nod.

I'm not sure what they're discussing, but it doesn't seem troubling since my little sister is smiling. She looks at me with a smile, reassuring me that everything's okay. She's always been honest with me, so if she's smiling, it's a good sign. And she won't deceive me, because she's the one who--

"Daddy, can we sleep together like usual?" I request, unsure how to convince him since we always sleep together.

Daddy silently lifts me and settles me in bed beside my little sister, allowing me to embrace her immediately despite my weakness. She hugs me back, and we stay like that, frozen in our embrace. I can't help but cry as memories flood back, and she comforts me with her gentle strokes.

"Please don't leave me again," I implore her. "I don't want to be without you."

"I'll do whatever it takes to see you smile again," she assures me.

Daddy watches us, pulls up a chair, and starts stroking us tenderly. His touch is so soothing that both my little sister and I instinctively reach out for more. He sighs and reassures us that everything will be fine now. I listen intently, feeling special for the first time—not in the way my little sister calls herself or how others refer to her at school, but truly special…

"You accepted me so quickly," Daddy remarks, stroking me gently, making me feel like purring. "Was it that tough?"

"My sister shielded me," I explain to him. "And she cried a lot, so I guess it was…"

"The little one wouldn't stand for it," remarks my little sister. "And I was expecting it. I was quite mean…"

"Don't speak ill of yourself," Daddy smiles sadly before continuing with his explanation.

Apparently, traces of medications linger in hair and nails for a long time, allowing one to identify the pills someone had consumed even years later. It turns out my little sister was given some prohibited pills, which explained her irritability and anger. The reason behind it remains unclear to me, but my little sister seems to understand. She starts sobbing, and then her tears flow silently. I hold her tightly, crying alongside her to ensure she doesn't cry alone.

"If she was given pills without being asked why she misbehaved, then it's not her fault for misbehaving! There's nothing to punish her for because it wasn't her fault!" That's what I tell Daddy, and he nods in agreement, wrapping us both in his arms. He holds us close, providing warmth and comfort. Nestled in his embrace, I feel as cozy as I do in my little sister's arms. I try not to dwell too much on Mommy and Daddy ascending to heaven—after all, it was their choice to go there, wasn't it? I also try not to think about being abandoned because I willingly exchanged myself for Mommy, just as my sister exchanged herself for me. Now I have a new Daddy, and maybe Mommy will be... well, if...

"Why?" asks my little sister, her tone slightly calmer. I'm not sure what she means, but Daddy seems to understand.

"There are no 'other people's children,'" he responds calmly. "You're sisters, and it's evident. You saved each other, didn't you?"

"She gave me more warmth than I've ever felt in my whole life," my little sister sobs, and hearing her words, even though I know she's had a difficult life, brings tears to my eyes.

She hasn't experienced those things firsthand; I've only told her about them. Yet, she speaks of it as if... I can't even find the words!

MUMMY, DADDY AND ALYONA

ELDER

Daddy Seryozha stays with us throughout the night, and we huddle together in Mashenka's room. It's peculiar, almost as if we're already in our own bodies. Logically, we shouldn't dream about each other, but we do. We sit together, embracing. Mashenka tells me how worried she was for me, how scared she felt. But our daddy turned out to be a very serious man, and I was quickly rescued. Now, Daddy promises not to separate us anymore.

Realizing that I may not have been to blame for my inexplicable anger, aggression... It's so challenging. But Dad's words... to call someone "Dad" without hesitation, without despair, but with the knowledge that you are loved—it's simply extraordinary, indescribable. I don't know how to react, how to take it all in, because I feel like crying all the time.

The morning starts with Dad dozing off and the door suddenly opening. Unsure of who it is, I instinctively shield my little sister with my arm, trying to protect her. But a woman in a bathrobe rushes into the room. She scans the room and then spots us. I try to rise to shield my sister further, but the woman leans over and scoops us both up.

"My darlings!" she whispers, kissing our faces. "You've suffered, my sweethearts... you were all alone... my darlings..."

She shows no preference between my little sister and me, lavishing kisses on each of us. I'm unsure of what's happening, and she seems on the verge of tears. She embraces us so tenderly... I lack the words to describe it. I've never been hugged like that before, so I don't even have any frame of reference. It's as if I'm enveloped in these arms, utterly oblivious to everything else.

"Hello, my darling," my father's voice reaches me, filled with such love that it's overwhelming. "Are you getting to know your daughters?"

"Didn't you say they were completely lost?" the woman snaps at him. "They need to be warmed up!"

"Who are you?" the little one asks timidly.

"I'm your mum, daughters," she replies, her tone uncertain. "From now on and forever, I'm your mum. What's wrong with them, Seryozha?"

"Here..." sighs our father. "I'll get used to it, for sure! We have to take her to us and sort it out, because the older one's story smells really bad."

"Lenka will be here in a minute," Mum says, holding us in her arms. "Let's get the little ones together... Or do they have to lie here?"

"We don't have to do that," Dad replies, looking at some paper. "We'll go to the embassy, that's what. Siegfried has promised to help."

"Good friends you have," she sighs, tucking us back in. "We'll wash up and have breakfast, and then Daddy will decide."

I'm confused by what's happening. These people accepted me instantly, as if I'd always been here, as if I'd always been their daughter. I don't understand it, and Mashenka clings to me, relying on my reactions. We've become true sisters during this time, as if we were born together.

Dad tells Mum about what he's learned, about how the younger one interprets it. I listen intently because everything feels strange. The little one seems fine, but me... Why wasn't I killed outright? It would have been simpler to just end my life, so why subject me to what they did? That's what baffles me. And with the youngest, it's even more unclear, but Daddy Seryozha is clearly troubled by what he's discovered.

It seems logical - the former lover of the girl's mum paid for the children's shelter. But here's the odd part... Dad mentions that the police and other serious individuals were searching for Mashenka, yet we were attending school and living in the children's shelter. Why the discrepancy?

That's what I can't wrap my head around because... Something doesn't add up here, and it's unsettling. Dad assures me it will be sorted out, so there's no need to worry. But my mum... Only now do I realize how different a real mum is from the one I had! Not only does she carry me in her arms, even though it's difficult, but she also envelops me in her soul in such a way that I'm utterly lost. I never imagined it could be like this.

"Daddy, Mummy!" A tall girl, older than me, likely in her twenties, bursts into the room.

Before I can fully see her, she's already by my side. I'm lying in bed, watching my little sister being washed through the open bathroom door, so I don't react immediately, but strangely, I don't panic either. The girl gazes at me with an odd look in her eyes, then simply smiles.

"Well, hello, sister," she says to me. "My name is Alyonka, in Russian. And you're Masha, right?"

"We're both named Masha," I inform her, noticing the surprise shadowing her face. "Are you sure you want to be my sister?"

"Daddy?" Alenka seems quite surprised already.

"She had a terrible life, my daughter," our father explains. "Very much so, and we don't know everything yet."

The new sister embraces me and reassures me that all the bad times are over now, because my parents will fix everything and she'll assist me. She assures me that I'll never be alone again, that all the bad things are in the past, and from now on, everything will be only good, because it has to be that way. I... I cry from her warmth, tenderness, and confidence. I want to believe her, but I'm also very scared because my entire life contradicts her words.

Then the youngest one appears, joining us. She immediately goes to hug Alenka, who carefully holds her in her arms. I don't see any hesitation in her eyes. Alyonka handles the youngest one very delicately, almost unaffected by her missing limbs, and it's quite puzzling to me. Speaking of the missing limbs...

"Daddy!" I call out to the adult, who instantly turns to me. "I need to get some covers for my little one's stumps because they make her cold and weepy. I tried to do something, but..."

"So that's what it was!" Dad realizes, then explains to Mum about the covers that were on the Younger's feet.

Our eldest sister seems on the verge of tears. I don't understand the reason for this, but I'm discovering strange things about myself. I feel like I'm suddenly regressing, which is totally unexpected for me. It's quite scary because how can I protect my little sister? I'm hesitant to completely trust adults, but they seem to understand... I wish I could comprehend everything like that...

Of all the things Dad has told us, I only understand about half of them, but...

YOUNGER

I don't really grasp adult conversations, but I try not to dwell on it because my little sister assures me that everything will be okay, just my legs... I avoid looking at... what's left of them because it makes me want to cry endlessly. I'll never run or jump again because I no longer have legs.

I understand now what my little sister shielded me from, but I can't hide in my room anymore. I need to adapt. Mummy... I have a mummy! She's even warmer and more attentive, very protective of me, not wanting to see me cry. I reminisce about the last month before my parents decided to leave for heaven. They seemed frustrated, maybe just worn out by me... Or did the sorcerer deceive Mum? It's too late to dwell on that now...

Mum washes us, starting with my little sister, then me. While she's washing me, it turns out we have a big sister! I wonder if we'll dream about her. Her name is Alyonka, and she already loves us, she claims! She joins us for breakfast, eager to help. Why should we need help? I can manage on my own! Oh... no, I can't...

"Why am I so weak?" I ask my sisters, feeling a bit scared.

"Because all the bad things are over," says the one who's Masha, not Alenka. "Everything's done, and you don't have to be strong anymore... Don't..."

She suddenly starts crying, and I join in, of course, because it's lonely for her to cry alone. But our eldest sister, Alyonka, embraces us both, urging us not to cry. How can you not cry if your sister is crying? And I'm there for her, but I can't cry for long because they bring breakfast. Daddy heads off on business, and Mum and Alyonka sit on either side of the bed to feed us. Masha, my sister, sighs as she understands everything.

"Shall we play a game?" she suggests to me. "As if you and I were very, very... small..." She hesitates, as if she's trying to swallow something, and Alyonka gazes at her anxiously, I can tell! "And we can't do it ourselves..."

"Let's!" I grin, pulling her closer into my arms. "Who's going to feed such good little girls?"

"We're going to feed you now!" Mum starts smiling. "Who's opening her mouth? Who's the best girl?"

I obediently open my mouth, as always, while Masha hesitates, unsure if it will hurt. We eat because we must, even though it's not appetizing. But we're in the hospital, where the food is always bland, so there's no point in being fussy, even though we really want to. With Mummy and my sister nearby, I feel like jumping, but there's nothing to jump on, so I settle for being a bit grumpy...

After breakfast, during which I don't dare misbehave because I feel scared for some reason, Mummy pauses and then asks Alyonka to fetch some socks. Sis nods, disappears briefly, then returns, holding something out to Mummy. They're socks, but they're big, ones I didn't have when...

when... Sensing I'm on the verge of tears, Masha hugs me and urges me not to cry.

"She felt warm, at ease," she explains to Alenka. "That's the realization she had..."

"And you?" Alenka asks.

"I've had it for a long time..." sighs Masha. "I didn't think..."

"She almost died, but her daddy saved her!" I interject, startling her. "And now she won't die..."

"And now we're going to put on our socks," Mummy says, and I feel her doing something, but my sisters are holding me, so I can't see.

Curious, I try to peek, but Masha, my sister, playfully holds me back, though I'm eager to see! Then I catch a glimpse - legs, or what's left of them, covered up, and I don't feel like crying at all. They don't look as scary or pathetic, so I smile.

"Thank you, Mummy!" I express my gratitude for the lovely gesture. "Very, very much!"

"Don't cry too much, baby," Mummy strokes my head. "Our daddy will figure something out for your legs."

Will he? This phrase makes me pause, wondering what to expect. But Mummy says it so confidently that I start to hope for a miracle, and I smile even more. It's reassuring to have caring adults around! And it's comforting not to cry... Plus, my little sister isn't crying either, because we're both receiving the same affectionate hugs now! Just as I'm beaming as much as I can, Daddy enters the room.

"Have the children eaten?" he asks Mummy. "Let's prepare them for transportation."

"Sweetheart?" Mummy inquires, to which Daddy responds that something isn't quite right, so he's called his friends over.

I don't grasp their conversation, but it doesn't seem necessary because Mom and Alyonka, my little sister, jump into action right away. Then more uncles and aunts enter the room, speaking a language I don't understand, but one of them hands Daddy a small red book. I'm unsure of its significance, but Alyonka seems to get it, clapping her hands in excitement.

Alenka is helping me get dressed, while Mom dresses Masha because she's older and can't manage on her own. I resist the urge to squirm to avoid getting in Alenka's way, although I really want to dress myself! But I refrain, understanding that I'm weak and it might take me a year to dress on my own, and why keep everyone waiting?

Masha instructs Alenka to be gentle with her legs, as they're still sensitive even after all this time. Mom and Dad exchange looks, and then Dad takes charge of me. I can tell Dad isn't entirely pleased, but he remains composed. I know what Dad Seryozha is like when he's not happy about something!

Once we're dressed, they scoop us up and carry us

towards the exit. Non-Russian-speaking uncles flank us, and I sense that something significant is happening, maybe even something scary, but I trust Mom, Dad, and Alyonka, so I'm not frightened. I just feel a bit uneasy, like there's something frightening, but at the same time, not really. Or is it? I'm not sure if it's frightening or not because they place me and my little sister into the car, and everyone is very solemn.

EMBASSY

ELDER

Suddenly, we find ourselves in a car, a dark blue minibus adorned with flags. I notice several cars ahead and behind us, with police officers standing in front. The adults appear tense, but they usher my little sister and me inside. Alyonka and her new mom sit beside us, while the driver and another man are up front with my dad.

Initially, they converse in a language I don't understand, and then the door opens again. The man beside my dad is handed a folder, and as the car lurches into motion, the door shuts behind us. The man reads the contents of the folder carefully, then bursts into laughter. Dad, seeming equally puzzled, takes the folder and eventually joins in the laughter.

"What's so funny?" our mom asks him, clearly perplexed.

"It's not straightforward with children," Dad explains.

"But whoever orchestrated this only deceived themselves. Remember when we heard about the little girl's parents?"

"Yeah," Mom nods, a hint of confusion in her expression. "So?"

"That's right," Dad chuckles. "The children don't have any local documents at all, you see."

"Where did they go?" Mom wonders aloud.

They switch to their own language, discussing something heatedly, but I've heard enough. It wasn't for nothing that the youngest called the "benefactor" a dreadful black sorcerer. If there are no documents on her, it suggests they were deliberately destroyed to erase her existence. Now I question if the accident was truly accidental. Could it be that one was intoxicated and the other caused a scene intentionally?

Being undocumented myself doesn't faze me anymore, but it's incredibly strange for my younger sister. It's all so baffling that I feel utterly lost. I'll need to ask Dad because right now, I understand nothing. And when I'm clueless, fear sets in. I dislike feeling afraid and being dependent on adults.

There must be something showing on my face because Mom suddenly interrupts her conversation with Dad and leans over to me. She gently strokes both mine and Younger's heads, calming us. I notice the youngest drifting off to sleep, but I can't relax completely because I feel responsible for protecting her.

. . .

"Your local documents have vanished," Mom whispers to me. "They're completely gone, so we couldn't locate Mashenka. However, she was registered as our daughter since we are her godparents, and that's sufficient for the German authorities. It was a bit more complicated with you, but since they couldn't find any documents for you either, we listed you as our daughter."

"What does that mean?" I ask, starting to grasp the situation. So far, I understand that both my youngest sister and I are considered Dad Seryozha's children. But the full implications elude me.

"And this, my daughter," Mom sighs, "means that we have two German girls, abducted by criminals, and the embassy guards are involved in their release and evacuation."

"So, does that mean we're safe?" I inquire, beginning to comprehend.

"Yes, little one," Dad confirms, nodding at me. "You're officially our daughters now, and there's no disputing that. But as for what exactly happened and why, the police, our authorities, and others will investigate."

I suddenly feel a sense of security. It dawns on me why there were so many police officers—they were searching for a foreign girl kidnapped by criminals. They found two, and now they'll look like heroes. Or maybe not. But that's not our concern at all. We'll have to learn the language and adapt to life in a new country. Hopefully, it's different from what we've experienced so far.

"What if the criminals try to attack?" I wonder, recalling Vaska.

"They wouldn't dare," Dad scoffs. "To attack an embassy convoy..."

I'm not familiar with the term "embassy convoy," but Dad's confidence reassures me that everything will be okay. Since the baby has fallen asleep, I should probably follow suit to keep her from feeling lonely. Plus, there's nothing happening, and Dad is conversing in an unfamiliar language again. I'm starting to realize how fortunate we both are. If it weren't for Dad's actions, we might have met a much darker fate. I've heard stories about people snatching children for organ harvesting... Maybe that's what was happening here too.

But it's still unclear to me... If they intended to sell me for parts, why did they medicate me? Maybe they wanted to save me somehow? Do I believe it? No, I don't... Gradually, I drift into sleep, somewhat convinced that we're out of harm's way now. Moreover, I notice we've left the city behind, so there's a long journey ahead, during which I can sit with the youngest one.

"Where have you been all this time?" She pouted when I woke up. "I've been waiting for so long!"

"Come here, sweetie," I comforted her, pulling her into a

tight hug. "We're safe now, and soon we'll be moving to a different country where things will be better."

"I believe you," the younger one whispered. "I believe everything will be okay, but my legs..."

"Mom said Dad would figure something out, remember?" I reassured her, and she nestled closer to me. Her eyes brimmed with hope.

"Do you think we'll dream about Sis too?" Masha asked me.

"I'm not sure about that," I chuckled.

We sat embracing each other, and my little sister asked me what I had realized. As I answered her, my thoughts raced. Many things that had happened seemed peculiar to me, and Ded Moroz wasn't the only mystery. He had simply placed me inside my little sister, saving her. The question lingered: why her? But I doubted I would ever know the answer. Nonetheless, she had saved herself, defying death numerous times... I believed the adults would uncover the truth, especially since our dad seemed extraordinary in this foreign land of Germany. One day, I felt we would unravel it all, perhaps sooner than I expected.

Not every citizen receives attention from the embassy, indicating there was something special about Dad. But it was a blessing because he rescued us, both of us, even when I had resigned myself to my fate. Now, there was a future, even for me, despite... Despite my condition. I chose to put my trust in Mom and Dad.

YOUNGER

I wake up as the car comes to a stop. Immediately, I notice the adults relaxing, indicating that we're in a safe place, free from any threats. They pick us up - Masha by Daddy and me by Mommy - and carry us inside. First, we enter a large grey building, then descend in an elevator. It keeps going until it finally stops. Glancing around, I see a corridor lined with doors. Mommy carries me past them until we reach a slightly open door. Then, something happens, and I find myself on the couch next to my little sister.

"The strollers will be brought in a little later," Daddy informs us. "While you two lie down and watch cartoons, I need to step out. Mommy and Alyona will stay with you, alright?"

"Deal," I agree, scanning the area for cartoons. The screen in front of the sofa lights up, playing one of my favorites about Tom the cat and Jerry the mouse. They chase each other around, but sometimes you feel sorry for Tom. Why can't they just be friends? Why all the chasing?

"When we get to Germany," Alenka says to me once the cartoon ends, "you'll go to school..."

"To school for..." Masha starts, unsure, but Alenka's surprised expression convinces me.

"To a regular school," she clarifies. "There will be extra help at first, especially for the little one, but it's a normal school."

"How normal? We're..." Masha can't believe it, and I don't want to remember what I saw in her memories.

"You two are very special," Alenka smiles. "You'll see for yourselves."

I'm not sure what "special" means, though I believe it. But for some reason, I feel like crying even more now. I wish I could be a baby again, to hide away. Mommy sighs and holds me close, rocking me gently, which soothes me. My big sister disappears briefly, then returns with some notebooks.

"Mom," she suggests. "How about I learn German with my sisters? It'll keep them occupied and cheer them up."

"That's a great idea," Mom approves, gently settling me back on the sofa. "Just take it easy, okay?"

"Of course," Sis agrees, getting down to business.

Learning a new language turns out to be very interesting. Both Masha and I find it enjoyable because we're not learning in a traditional classroom setting, but rather through play. Alyonka helps me with letter and word memorization and sings songs, making time fly by unnoticed until it's time for lunch. They bring us strollers - one for me with wheels I can spin myself, and one with a handle for my sister. They put us both in, explaining to her what she needs, while Mom assists me, even though I can manage on my own.

"It must be difficult for our middle daughter to spin the wheels by herself," my mom explains to me. "That's why she has a stroller with a motor, so she can drive herself. Now, let's head to the canteen..."

And off we go to the canteen, bustling with people. There are military personnel and others in identical suits seated separately. However, everyone who sees us smiles and greets us, and I return the greetings with a smile. After all, my mom explained to me that I'll be a German girl now, just like my sisters, so I need to get used to it.

"Oh, here are our heroic girls!" exclaims a chubby man with an accent, catching my attention.

"Why are we heroic?" I ask.

"Because you survived," the man responds seriously. "Survived and helped us find some very bad people."

As I settle at the table, I ponder. "Very bad people," it sounds like something terrible was going to happen to us. Maybe to eat me, and perhaps just to harm my little sister. So she had her own scary black sorcerer, and those sorcerers were somehow connected. Well, we're connected, so the sorcerers must be too, right?

Now we're allowed to eat on our own, but I'm surprised by the way lunch is served: salad first, then the main course, but no appetizer. And the dessert is unusual. Everything is so intriguing, yet strange! I pick up my fork and begin to eat, noticing that it's a bit difficult for my sister Masha to handle hers.

"Mom! Sis needs help!" I call Mom's attention to it.

"Yes, my daughter," Mom sighs. "Your little sister is struggling in the snow, and she's not used to asking for help. Come on, Mashenka," she addresses her little sister, not me. "Let me help you."

"Herr Doctor," a military man approaches our table. "The Russians are providing a hospital plane; it will depart in two hours."

"Why all of a sudden?" Dad wonders, setting down his fork.

"It's a collective effort," the military man sighs. "The sooner the children are safe, the easier it will be to proceed."

"That's correct," Dad nods, turning to us. "You heard him," he smiles. "Let's finish eating quickly and head home."

I don't fully grasp what the man and Dad were discussing, but they spoke Russian, probably so we could understand and not be frightened. It's reassuring to be looked after! I gather that we're going home now because the man said so, and everything will be okay there, I suppose. Dad seemed happy about it, and someone mentioned safety. That means we'll be away from the scary black sorcerers, and they won't harm me anymore.

So I try to eat swiftly to not hold anyone up. Mom also speeds up a bit since I still need to pack... Oh. I have nothing to pack because all my belongings are left at the children's shelter. How will I manage without everything? Should I go back to the children's shelter to retrieve my things? Or maybe not, because the witches might be there?

"I left everything at the children's shelter," I mention with uncertainty.

"We'll get new things at home," Mom reassures me. "Since grandfather is..."

"Not a good one, huh?" I inquire.

"Yes, dear," Mom strokes my head, and I feel calmer.

My mom and dad chose to depart to heaven and create another Mashenka there who wouldn't upset them, but I have my parents and sisters here, so I'm fine without them. I've shed enough tears over their departure. In my little sister's embrace, I grieved over it, but why cry over the same thing twice?

ERROR MANAGEMENT

ELDER

"Mom! Sis needs help!" I call Mom's attention to it.

"Yes, my daughter," Mom sighs. "Your little sister is struggling in the snow, and she's not used to asking for help. Come on, Mashenka," she addresses her little sister, not me. "Let me help you."

"Herr Doctor," a military man approaches our table. "The Russians are providing a hospital plane; it will depart in two hours."

"Why all of a sudden?" Dad wonders, setting down his fork.

"It's a collective effort," the military man sighs. "The sooner the children are safe, the easier it will be to proceed."

"That's correct," Dad nods, turning to us. "You heard him," he smiles. "Let's finish eating quickly and head home."

I don't fully grasp what the man and Dad were discussing, but they spoke Russian, probably so we could understand and not be frightened. It's reassuring to be looked after! I gather that we're going home now because the man said so, and everything will be okay there, I suppose. Dad seemed happy about it, and someone mentioned safety. That means we'll be away from the scary black sorcerers, and they won't harm me anymore.

So I try to eat swiftly to not hold anyone up. Mom also speeds up a bit since I still need to pack... Oh. I have nothing to pack because all my belongings are left at the children's shelter. How will I manage without everything? Should I go back to the children's shelter to retrieve my things? Or maybe not, because the witches might be there?

"I left everything at the children's shelter," I mention with uncertainty.

"We'll get new things at home," Mom reassures me. "Since grandfather is..."

"Not a good one, huh?" I inquire.

"Yes, dear," Mom strokes my head, and I feel calmer.

My mom and dad chose to depart to heaven and create another Mashenka there who wouldn't upset them, but I have my parents and sisters here, so I'm fine without them. I've shed enough tears over their departure. In my little sister's embrace, I grieved over it, but why cry over the same thing twice?

Gradually, I comprehend what Daddy is explaining. The

discomfort... Mashenka's leg issues... and my near immobility, only managing to use the bathroom by myself - it's all intentional. Moreover, both Mashenka and I share the same mother, but she abandoned me, while the younger one stayed. Now it's clear why I lived in her, in my opinion. Since we're sisters, we share a blood bond; that's probably the reason. Daddy mentions something about Santa Barbara, if I heard correctly, then steps away again to clarify something, he says.

It's evening, so we'll likely be fed and then put to bed. It's saddening, of course, that they did this to me and the youngest, but there's nothing to be done now, I suppose. Perhaps we can find a way to comfort her... And we'll need to talk to her to help her come to terms with herself, as it's challenging for her.

I feel sorrowful; it seems there were no decent people there at all, not even during the operation... So was everything planned? But I'm alive, and though I can't feel anything below my waist, I guess I can manage... I want to cry, but I can't because my little sister would understand and cry too, and it's not good for her; she's losing consciousness for a reason.

Dad and some other doctors enter the room. They approach me first, stroke my head, and through Mom, ask permission to examine me. They do! Me! They don't just examine me without consent! I'm close to tears!

"Shh, shh..." Mom observes everything. She strokes my

head and explains something to the doctors, who shake their heads, looking at me sympathetically.

Then they turn me over and start examining me, conversing among themselves. And I, already tensing up in anticipation of the cold, gradually relax because the doctors' hands are warm. They discuss among themselves, there's some rustling, but no aggression in their voices; they debate, I can sense it in their tones, but they do so quietly. Then they turn me back over, and my dad sits down beside the bed.

"Daughter, we can't fully repair your legs," he begins, looking me directly in the eye. "But we can partially restore sensation. You'll be able to feel when you need to use the bathroom, for example... We have specialized wheelchairs that can help you stand up, but we can't fully fix it."

"Daddy... Mommy..." I sob because even the simple act of going to the bathroom independently is a dream I've had to let go of. And Daddy also mentions that when I grow up, I'll have a partner... I'll have... A partner like that?

"What monsters..." Mom sighs, stroking my head.

Then the doctors move on to the little sister. They also seek permission as they examine Masha, who whimpers, while Alyonka soothes her, diverting her attention from their actions. Nodding to each other, the doctors depart, but Daddy remains with us. He gazes at me attentively, then at Mashenka, and smiles.

"Now, my dears, it's time to sleep," he tells us. "And when you wake up, things will be much better."

I realize that we're probably going to be treated while we sleep now, undoing what the... others have done. But I beckon my dad to ask him why. Why they did this to us. Yet he strokes my head, reassuring me that everything has its time, and I believe him. I believe that we'll be informed of everything, and it will get easier. For both me and Mashenka, because everything is very delicate there, and it hurts, and prosthetics probably aren't an option. Truly, it turns out, they're beasts...

The nurse enters with a smile, explaining through Mom that we'll receive a small injection soon and then drift off to sleep without feeling anything. I wonder why it's happening today. Is it really so urgent? I ask Mom this, attempting to grasp her response. I try to understand, but it doesn't quite register.

"They don't want to delay your treatment," Mom reassures me. - The hospital operates round the clock, and the professor believes the sooner, the better.

As I lie there, I ponder about this amazing country where doctors genuinely care about people like me.

YOUNGER

When I spot my little sister in my room, I rush over to her eagerly. Now she'll explain everything to me because I'm feeling so lost! She embraces me right away as I bounce around her. But now, jumping is only possible in my dreams. The thought saddens me.

"Don't be sad!" Masha commands. - "You'll jump again, because there's a secret."

"What secret?" I wonder, trying to imagine myself jumping.

"What kind of secret would it be if I told you?" she teases, squinting at me.

I give her puppy-dog eyes, and Masha sighs, then starts explaining about these high boots that almost resemble feet. You put them on, and you can even jump. It sounds like a fairy tale, but I believe my sister, so I hold onto hope. But I'm eager to know more than just about the boots because I didn't grasp anything from what Dad told me, so I urge Masha to tell me more.

"We're sisters," she explains, her eyes filled with sadness. - "Your mom, Dad said, she's... She's my mom too."

"She left you," I nod, understanding dawning upon me. - "But she wanted me too because the sorcerer had cast a spell. He must have done it before, right?"

"I guess," she smiles back at me. - "We're undergoing surgery now, so you won't be in so much pain, and I... So I can feel when I sit, you know?"

"I see..." I reply, contemplating. - "Are they fixing what they did before now?"

"Yes, little one," she nods.

Masha tells me that "there," they did everything wrong, but probably for a reason because it turns out they wanted to dismantle us for spare parts. I don't grasp it immediately, and when my sister explains in detail, I start crying. Not because they wanted to dismantle me, but because the sorcerer probably planned to sell me in pieces to other sorcerers. It's terrifying to realize that they just wanted to chop me up and sell me like a chicken...

Daddy didn't just rescue me from longing and pain; he saved me from something much worse. And he saved Masha too. Now we'll be alright because Daddy will defeat all those scary black sorcerers. They won't exist anymore, and we're not scared of them because we're in another country. Here, they don't want to hurt or torture, and it turns out hitting your bottom isn't allowed at all! And no one does it... "There," it was forbidden too, but it didn't stop anyone, but here it does!

It's challenging for me to adjust because my sister shares such unsettling things about "there"... It seems like it'll be the same here, but for now, everything indicates we're safe at home. But what lies ahead, I don't know. But my little sister confidently assures me that everything will be fine now, and I believe her. It's Masha! She can't be wrong!

I wake up slowly, as if reluctant to. I don't feel any pain, which is strange because last time I woke up, it hurt a lot.

Masha was nearly crying nonstop then, so it must have hurt a lot, but I don't feel any pain now. I wonder why?

As I open my eyes, I see my mom smiling at me. I know my little sister will wake up soon, so I turn my head slowly in her direction to see her sleepy eyes. She's the one who saved me day and night, who comforted me when I was sad or scared... And when I didn't understand what was happening too.

Dad arrives with two doctors, and it turns out they've not only fixed my sister's back but also her heart. And mine too, because there was something wrong hidden in there that they found and fixed. Now, I won't unexpectedly fall asleep anymore, and my little sister won't have to be scared because her heart is better now.

We need to stay here for a few days, and then my sister and I can go home. We'll rest and study so we can go back to school after the holidays. I almost forgot that New Year's Eve is coming! I wonder how it's celebrated here. Even though I've probably already received all the presents, I still want the holiday, the joy, and the hope... I just want to see my parents smiling... I really, really want it!

"Dad, why doesn't it hurt?" I ask. "Shouldn't it hurt after surgery?"

"No, my daughter," Dad says. "It shouldn't hurt, and we'll make sure it doesn't anymore."

"I felt like I went into a fairy tale," my little sister whispers, and I hold her hand to show her she's alive.

"You didn't die, dear," Mom smiles sadly at her. "Now you don't have to be strong and face the world alone. You're our child, and children shouldn't be hurt."

"The baby..." my sister whispers. "Can I cry?"

"You can," Dad nods. "But not too much, we don't want to stress the heart. We've treated you, but we're still being cautious..."

It's already morning, and soon they'll bring us food and water. It's important to eat to regain strength. The New Year is coming soon, and we hope to be fully recovered in time to enjoy it. Even if we're in wheelchairs, we can still find happiness! So, I'll try very hard to recover because I really want to be happy and celebrate!

It's sad that my mom left Masha when she was born... But she left me too. So, I'll be obedient and believe they're doing well wherever they are. Dad Seryozha was always there for me, caring and supportive. He's a real dad.

Alenka says my sister and I are bored lying around, so we're learning German together. We practice words, and it's a lot of fun!

Despite everything, I have my little sisters and my family. I'll never be abandoned again.

Alenka noticed that my sister and I were getting bored lying around, so she suggested we practice German together. She points out words in pictures, and we repeat them after her. First, I say the word, then Masha does, because that's the proper way. Alenka corrects us and then suggests playing a word game later. We take turns saying a word in Russian, and she translates it into German, and vice versa. It's incredibly enjoyable, just a lot of fun!

Despite the sadness at times, I'm grateful for how things turned out. I have my little sisters, my family, and I know I'll never, ever be abandoned again!

SOMEWHERE FAR AWAY

DED MOROZ OFFICE

DED MOROZ WAS TROUBLED by several things. It could have been the peculiar letter from his Western counterpart, Santa Claus, inquiring about information transfer, or perhaps the missing staff, or even Snow Maiden's unusual behavior. The wording of the letter from Ded Moroz was rather peculiar, especially the phrase "torturing children enough," which left Ded Moroz perplexed. He couldn't fathom why he would be accused of such a thing. So, he decided to have a conversation with the Snow Maiden first.

"Granddaughter," Grandpa began affectionately, then adopted a more stern tone, "is there something you need to tell me?"

The girl, around twelve years old, looked away, betraying herself.

"I'd prefer to hear the news from you, not from Santa Claus," Ded Moroz said sternly but wearily.

"Well," the Snow Maiden mumbled, assuming a defensive posture.

Further inquiry unraveled a rather puzzling situation, which Ded Moroz couldn't immediately comprehend. However, after summoning the trainee responsible for the chaos, Grandfather began unraveling the events. On one hand, it seemed the young assistant had stolen the staff to cause trouble, but on the other hand, there was more to the story. Despite the long-standing rule against interfering in people's affairs on New Year's Eve, something was different this time.

"The little girl was supposed to be killed," the assistant explained tearfully, realizing the potential reward for his recklessness. "But she's my sister..."

Ded Moroz muttered thoughtfully, reflecting on his own past experiences of intervening in similar situations.

"There were no consequences for the wrongdoing! None!" the Snow Maiden exclaimed. "So, everything is justified!"

"Indeed," the elderly man nodded, tugging at his beard thoughtfully.

This time, people had crossed a line that transcended the boundaries of good and evil, and Ded Moroz was displeased with the outcome. The girls had survived against the odds, though it seemed impossible, but one couldn't undo what had been done. If there was no retribution, it indicated a will greater than that of the New Year's spirit. However, leaving it unresolved wasn't an option.

"Why didn't you restore their legs?" Ded Moroz inquired.

"I attempted, but it was unsuccessful," the assistant sighed, wiping his eyes.

"Very well, I'll handle it," the mystical old man declared.

Gazing into a snowflake-filled globe, he pondered how humanity allowed such atrocities. Within the sphere, he saw numerous figures in distinct uniforms, apprehending others, and sometimes resorting to violence. Some sought wealth, orchestrating elaborate schemes to traffic... children. It was beyond comprehension, though Ded Moroz had witnessed worse in his centuries of existence. Each time, he grappled with the enormity of it.

The old man's eyes reflected weary children longing for lost loved ones, some pleading for their own lives, yet matters of life and death were beyond his control. Before him loomed gray walls erected by oppressors, impassable barriers. He witnessed children succumbing to dire illnesses, over which he held no sway.

Gifts for the virtuous, naught for the wicked—it seemed simple. Yet, at times, understanding eluded him. The young assistant had acted hastily, albeit rightly, saving the lives of two girls and exposing the horrors overlooked by society. The gravity of their indifference weighed heavily. Still, the girls deserved a parting gift from Ded Moroz, now that they resided in a different realm. It was a gift worth negotiating for.

Leaving the cottage where the young, innocent souls pondered their deeds, Ded Moroz settled into his sleigh and commanded the reindeer. He needed to visit Santa Claus; after all, the girls were now in his jurisdiction. It wasn't merely an ethical concern; the laws of New Year functioned differently in the West, making Christmas the primary holiday there.

Santa Claus appeared expectant as his eastern counterpart arrived. With a warm smile, he welcomed Ded Moroz into his home, offering tea and sweets before inquiring about the fate of the two girls. The magical old man proceeded to recount the girls' story to his colleague. Ded Moroz understood Santa Claus' limited capacity for compassion, yet he didn't seek to evoke pity. He simply wished to offer a parting gift.

Santa Claus wasn't originally from this region; he had been brought here by others, but now he was in charge. He listened intently to his counterpart from the East and nodded in understanding.

"It makes sense," replied the Western minister of Christmas. "So, you'll restore the younger one's legs, grant the older one the ability to walk, and I'll ensure everyone believes that's what happened, but..."

"Just regaining their legs isn't enough; they need to learn how to use them," Ded Moroz interjected.

"That's the tricky part," Santa chuckled. "It's something they have to figure out for themselves. They have doctors; all they need is determination, you know?"

"You're simplifying things," Ded Moroz grinned. "Well, suit yourself. It's better than nothing at all... Can I inform them?"

"Feel free to tell them as much as you like," chuckled his Western counterpart.

There was still ample time before New Year's Eve, a time known for bringing miracles to many families. The streets remained unlit, and Santa's sack wasn't yet brimming with presents. The Snow Maiden and her young assistant, still unnamed, were perplexed. Little did they realize that despite breaking numerous rules and laws, they had done the right thing. Hence, there was no severe punishment.

As New Year's Eve approached, the Snow Maiden and her companion, spared from a deserved scolding, were astonished. Ded Moroz didn't commend them specifically for the staff incident but praised their overall conduct. The girl, though centuries old, remained the same spirited troublemaker. This time, however, their mischief had been justified. Ded Moroz shared this revelation with his young helpers, leaving them both bewildered.

"But if you pull a stunt like that on me again!" he warned, shaking his staff.

A rooster figurine on the staff detached, gleaming in the sunlight, revealing Ded Moroz's true sentiments. The Snow Maiden and her companion smiled upon seeing it, but the magical old man only sighed. Children would always be children.

SPECIAL INVESTIGATIVE TASK FORCE

"Black market organ traffickers, Major," the investigator from the team responded concisely. "Interpol's involvement suggests it's serious."

"But have they vanished from our grasp?" questioned Major Zamorzaev, a specialist in high-profile cases.

"It's too early to determine," sighed his subordinate.

The fire erupted in December, just before the New Year festivities. While locals had grown somewhat accustomed to an Interpol officer scouring the country for his missing daughter, the discovery of her, and the subsequent tales, rattled nerves. Rumors spread like wildfire, prompting the chief of police in a coastal town to shake in his boots. It was one thing when a local girl vanished, but quite another when two disabled girls, now equipped with German documents instead of local ones, entered the picture. The situation escalated rapidly, drawing in state security authorities, who were unyielding in their pursuit of justice. This wasn't a matter of threatening a doctor and his family or attempting to buy someone off; it had become an international affair.

With the involvement of a special investigative team, surprises abounded, necessitating immediate security measures for the investigators and their families. It felt like a return to the tumultuous nineties, with a sprawling network operating across borders, leaving a staggering number of victims in its wake.

"If it weren't for those girls, we might never have uncovered any of this," lamented the Major.

"And the fact that the children miraculously survived..." the subordinate added as a reminder.

Two orphanages, one of them private, and a children's shelter were all part of the traffickers' network, supplying organs from living bodies. In some cases, relatives were murdered to obtain the organs needed. However, the mastermind behind it all was not within the country; the operation's strings were pulled from abroad. Now, it was up to Interpol to track down the primary orchestrator, and they pursued the trail with unwavering determination. There was hope that the main culprit would soon be apprehended.

Besides uncovering the organ transplant network, investigators also found troubling details about the failures of social services, schools, doctors, and the police. Even those not bribed by the criminals had something to answer for. The investigator looked into the eyes of the rescued children. Apart from the two German girls who initiated the investigation, there were also five boys and seven girls rescued. Though deeply affected by the loss of their loved ones, they could still be helped. Psychologists, psychiatrists, and foster families were capable of helping these young people recover.

One thing puzzled the investigator - how did these two sisters manage to stay strong? Despite their ordeal, they held onto each other tightly. Perhaps that's why they survived.

The investigator didn't have an answer, but there was still much to be done. They needed to apprehend everyone involved, examine each case individually, and uncover the reasons for such complicity. Meanwhile, the investigator pondered the resilience of the two girls who hadn't crumbled despite their traumatic experiences. How did they manage it?

"Let's see," he muttered, reopening the case. "Masha, fourteen years old... Artificially induced aggression, stop! She's not fit for transplant with these drugs!"

Suddenly, the investigator realized what had been bothering him. They needed to investigate the connections of the girl's former guardians to determine why she had been given these harmful substances. The artificially induced aggression and the abuse at home must have contributed to her distrust of adults and her violent tendencies, which were different from the other victims.

Work began to uncover the root causes. Discovering who and why had made the girl unsuitable for the criminals was crucial. In the opinion of the investigator, it could unveil the truth and approach the network from a different angle. Getting closer to the truth was paramount because, through the investigation's sieve, someone might slip away. The investigator was determined to eradicate this contagion from its root.

Less than a week later, citizen Sinichkin, who had attempted to enter the late guardians' apartment, was apprehended. He wasn't a professional thief, so under pressure, he confessed. His words, written on paper, were damning, making everyone involved wish to wash their hands. This time, the girl was to be used to extort money from her biological father. But even after that, the freaks wouldn't leave the child alone, disregarding her young age of only fourteen.

Nostalgically, I recalled the wild '90s, when such lawlessness seemed somewhat understandable. With a deep sigh, I started heading home. All that was left was to tie up loose ends, apprehend the last suspects, and, despite the inner turmoil, extract from them the location of the underground brothel. The Major struggled to fully trust in the impartiality of the legal system, so he often found himself taking on the roles of both prosecutor and judge. It wasn't entirely lawful, but he believed it was the right thing to do.

Meanwhile, far away, two girls were attempting to leave their past behind like a nightmare. They cared little about being victimized by criminals or the varying nature of people. Instead, they were stepping into their childhood, aiming to live it the way it was meant to be, untouched by bandits and murderers. This chapter of the girls' lives had been closed.

NEW YEAR

ELDER

We're discharged from the hospital on New Year's Eve! We're not fully healed yet; even the stitches are still in place. But Dad takes responsibility and arranges for us to celebrate the New Year at home, and it happens. We leave the hospital and Dad drives us home in his spacious car. It's big, almost like a minibus, with side doors that slide open. There's a special child seat for Mashenka in the center at the back, with me sitting on her right and Alenka on her left.

It takes us about an hour to reach home from the hospital. Our house has six apartments and three floors, not far from the bus stop, and surrounded by greenery—although now it's all covered in snow. As the car turns into our driveway, Mashenka lets out a little shriek.

We discover that our garage is underground. Dad parks

the car and then takes out the strollers to move us into them. Suddenly, we realize there's an elevator in our three-story house! It seems unbelievable, surprising both Mashenka and me. It feels like we're in a fairy tale, something I haven't felt in a while.

"Dad, Mashenka probably wants to share a room with me, right?" I ask, trying to sound confident. "We have a room for each of us, but..."

"I want to be with my sister!" Mashenka immediately declares. "Please don't separate us..."

"She's scared to be alone," I explain, reaching over to comfort her, then adding quietly, "And so am I..."

"Don't worry," Mom says, smiling affectionately at us. "We already thought about that."

It turns out our parents prepared our room while we were in the hospital, although it doesn't seem like they were gone at all. We slowly settle into our room. Looking around, I see greenish wallpaper, two wardrobes, beds with matching handles, a table, and even chairs. It all feels warm and cozy. Oh, and there's a vanity table with mirrors—a touch that tells me this room belongs to girls!

"How beautiful..." Mashenka whispers, and I feel tears welling up.

Comparing this to what I had as a child—the old sofa, the worn-out table, the rickety wardrobe—it's like night and day. Mashenka's room was just as nice, but I always assumed it was because her parents were wealthy. I'll have to find out more about our family's financial situation—what we can dream of and what we can't—but that's a question for later.

The youngest sibling asks about the beds, and then Mom starts showing us how to use all the equipment. Each bed has a button in the bathroom and toilet, so we can call for help. It's incredibly simple. And all these handles—each one is for us to be able to get into bed by ourselves, to move from the stroller, and just for... Parents who thought about our need for a little independence... It's indescribable; it can only be felt. My youngest sibling and I rush to thank our parents.

But the most important thing is that I can feel my underwear and that I'm sitting too. And even going to the toilet... They took off my diaper and helped me put on normal panties. Normal ones, in pink and white stripes, feel like a miracle, an impossible miracle. I can feel them against my skin —an almost forgotten sensation. And I can feel so much more, things that make me want to cry because the emotions are overwhelming.

The doctors, in my opinion, performed a miracle—I can't feel my legs, of course, but I can feel everything else perfectly! And my mom was surprised to find out that I didn't have the same days as everyone else, but I didn't. They examined me back at the hospital... well, between my legs... and said that they didn't hurt me too badly when they hit me, and I didn't have my days because of some pills that made me angry. Now the pills are gone, so those days will come, and I have to be prepared for them. Mom explained everything to me back at the hospital, so I know where the pads are and what to do when it hurts. And it will likely hurt because of being beaten as a child. I don't really understand what that has to do with it.

But what really surprises me is the toys. Dolls... At first, I think they're just for the youngest, but Mom says, "your dolls." What does she mean, ours? I'm not supposed to have any more, I'm big now, right?

"You need toys, my daughter, at any age," Mom sighs. "Adults have theirs, children have theirs. Here we have stuffed toys..."

And I cling to a big soft fluffy dog, dark brown with a white triangle on his chest and white paws. I'm just holding onto it, hugging it, and next to me, my little sister is doing the same with a huge bear. For a while, we're both lost in our own world, with Mom nodding understandingly.

Yes, we have each other, but sometimes I just want to... and the younger one does too, I know she does. And Mom says it's okay. But then I remember that we have to decorate the Christmas tree, so I remind my youngest, and we reluctantly leave our room.

"Do you like it?" Dad asks, watching us closely.

We're bringing in toys, and Mashenka's got this huge bear —it's like a giant!

"It's amazing," I reply honestly. "Are we going to decorate the tree?"

"Of course," Dad confirms. "We'll trim the tree while everything's cooking, and then we'll celebrate."

"And... what about me?" my youngest sister asks quietly, looking at Dad hopefully.

I remember she didn't get to celebrate New Year's Eve, even though she really wanted to. But her celebration was postponed until morning, and our parents always made sure to be there for her. I'm not sure how much they were at fault for the accident. Dad said the car might have been faulty, but I've seen more than just that one day. Dad, who once told Mashenka he'd leave her someday. Mom, who went "left," and it seems it wasn't the first time, considering I was an orphan. It's all complicated, but Mashenka had a happy childhood, and she'll continue to have one, because legs aren't everything —it's about the attitude. We're both loved, even though we're different. They call us special, which means our childhood isn't over yet, and for some of us, it's just beginning.

YOUNGER

Our room feels magical! I adore it, especially the bear. It's just like the one I used to have! I thought I'd lost him forever, but here he is, waiting for me. It's exactly the same bear, even smells the same. I know Daddy saved him for me, just like he saved me and my little sister. Daddy can do anything!

My parents have made it possible for us to do things on

our own now. I can even move from the bed to the pram by myself! It's such a miracle, I can't put it into words. But we can't stay in the room for too long because we have a Christmas tree waiting for us. It's not decorated yet, and I wonder why.

"Because the whole family has to decorate it together," my mum explains. "And our two youngest daughters were in the hospital, so it waited for you."

My sister and I can't help but cry at the thought of the tree waiting for us. It's almost unbearable to think of missing out on decorating it together. In the past, I always decorated the tree with my parents, except for the time I was sick. They decorated it themselves then, so as not to miss celebrating the New Year.

"What if we hadn't made it to New Year's Eve?" I ask, curious.

"Then the Christmas tree wouldn't be decorated," Alenka giggles. "Being together is what matters. Always!"

Her words make me cry even more, but this time with relief. It's just impossible to imagine decorating the tree without everyone there. I realize then that my parents are truly extraordinary, like angels sent from heaven to comfort us and love my little sister, who is simply wonderful.

Once we've dried our tears, we get to work decorating the tree. Masha and I start from the bottom, while Alyonka, Mum, and Dad start from the top, agreeing to meet in the middle. I remember to hang the heavier decorations lower down and tell Masha, since she's never decorated a tree before. It's a whole new experience for my dear little sister, and I'm thrilled to share it with her.

Then Daddy lifts me up to put the star on top, and our Christmas tree, so colorful, is finally ready. It's adorned with glittering ornaments and artificial snow sprayed on its branches, and two garlands shimmer beautifully. I gaze at the tree, reminiscing about last New Year's Eve, and I realize that only happiness lies ahead, even though I'm in a pram. The tree is so beautiful that nothing bad can happen.

"Now mum and dad are going to prepare food," Alenka informs me. "And you and I are going to watch movies!"

"What movies?" I ask, surprised, as usually I have to wait quietly until evening to watch anything.

"You'll see!" she says, with a mischievous smile, guiding us over to the sofa and seating us down.

I guess Alenka wants to treat us both, so she puts on Russian films. "I've seen Morozko, but not the second one, about Masha and Vitya. At home, we had different films - about the Grinch, Christmas spirits, and so on, but here it's entirely different. Alyonka says our daddy loves 'Soviet' films, but I'm not sure what they are. They must be special."

As we watch the children venture into Baba-Yaga's clutches, I share with Alenka about the scary black sorcerer I encountered, who almost cast a spell on Mum. But he only took a bit from me. Alenka hugs both Masha and me, silently comforting us with her warm embrace. It speaks volumes without a single word.

We watch magical films that inspire me to believe in Daddy's magic and reassure me that everything will be alright. And then... and then... and then... and then...

I'm allowed to celebrate New Year's Eve with everyone! Not just "we'll celebrate in the morning," but to celebrate together, just like adults! This news fills me with joy, and I can't help but squeal in happiness. Mummy and Daddy, along with Masha and Alenka, stroke me affectionately, understanding why I'm so overjoyed. It's very important to me now to celebrate New Year's Eve together with everyone. Maybe because I've been shown that we do everything together? I don't have the answer, but it doesn't matter because it's New Year's Eve!

Then I have to rest a bit so I don't fall asleep at the table. Masha joins me in bed for company, and Alyonka stays close to help if needed, although the handles and loops are quite helpful... I can manage on my own! Masha needs a bit of assistance, so Alenka helps her, and soon we drift off to sleep, looking forward to reuniting in my old room.

"How about we make this our room?" I suggested to my little sister.

"Let's do it! - she beams at me.

We begin redecorating... I run my hand over the pale, translucent toys, cupboards, and beds one last time before they vanish, and then the two of us start transforming it into our bedroom. Wardrobes, bedside tables, and beds start appearing... It's odd, I never asked Dad what happened to my old things from the old flat. I should probably ask him later....

We barely finish before we're called to the table, realizing it's already eleven o'clock at night! Alyonka helps me put on a beautiful dress, a light blue one with sparkling stars, while Masha gets the same dress but in green, which complements her eyes - at least that's what Mum says.

"You look so beautiful!" I tell Masha, but she looks in the mirror and starts crying again. I don't understand why she's crying; I don't feel like crying at all.

"You look beautiful too," she smiles through her tears.

"Why are you crying?" I ask her, but Alenka answers for her.

"It's just emotions," she explains. "Masha really likes the dress, so she's emotional, you know?"

I understand because I feel the same emotions, but we're expected at the festive table, so we all dress up. There's a lot of food - salads, sandwiches, and Masha and I even get champagne! It's the children's kind, from a colorful bottle, but it feels so grown-up! Dad raises his glass, making a toast, wishing that the passing year takes away all the sorrows but leaves behind the joys, and I couldn't agree more... Really, really couldn't.

A PRESENT FROM DED MOROZ

ELDER

WE'RE GATHERED around the festive table... It's a sensation I've never felt before, both thrilling and unsettling, like a dream come true. It feels surreal, as if it never happened before and will keep happening from now on, just as my dad says. Every day, every hour, I feel closer to Mum and Dad, as if they've always been mine. It's like everything before was just a nightmare, and now I'm finally back home, with Mum and Dad.

"It's almost five minutes to midnight," Dad smiles. "Is everyone's glass filled?"

"Mine is!" Alenka chirps back.

Then something amazing happens, in my opinion. Dad lifts Mashenka in his arms, handing her a glass, while Mum lifts me up, wrapping her arms around my waist. Everyone stands up, and as the clock strikes twelve... it's like a fairytale! I've been crying a lot lately...

The clock strikes midnight, glasses clink, we all take a sip, and smiles light up our faces because the moment feels truly magical. Then they gently set me down, and Dad is about to say something when two unexpected guests enter the room. Oh, Ded Moroz... please don't take me away! Please! I'll be good, I promise!

"Don't be frightened, child," Ded Moroz reassures me, and I can't recognize the other man beside him. Is it the Snow Maiden who changed her appearance? "No one is taking you away."

Tears stream down my face from the fear I felt, everyone hugs me tightly, and I can't stop crying because I never want to be without my family. I've only just started to live, not like before...

"Meet Santa Claus, by the way," Ded Moroz introduces. "Since you've moved, this will be the last time we see you."

"Who are you, uninvited guest?" Dad asks politely.

"He's Ded Moroz, Daddy," I reply between sobs. "A real one..."

"Real, indeed," Dad says, unsurprised. "What brings you here?"

"Your younger children have been through a lot," Ded Moroz begins. "The eldest has changed her perspective on life, and the youngest has remained strong. We'd like to give them a gift."

"I suppose it's more than just that," Mum grins.

"It's not just that," Santa Claus confirms. "But that's not important right now."

"We've decided you're deserving of a gift..." Ded Moroz taps his staff on the floor, and suddenly...

My youngest sister starts squealing with joy, and I'm so startled for her that I jump up from my seat... I'm standing! My legs wobble, and I fall back into my seat, but I can feel them, and... I was standing! I'm not sure what's happening, I touch my legs and start crying because they're there! I can feel them, and when I look over, I see that my little sister has legs too! Real ones!

A moment later, both of us erupt in a mixture of cries and shouts, releasing all the emotions tied to our past - the orphanage, the wheelchairs, the medical verdict... The baby reaches out for me, and we embrace each other, crying out loud in disbelief at what just happened. We have legs! We have legs! We can walk! We...

Our parents embrace us, trying to soothe us, but it's futile. We just can't seem to stop, and Ded Moroz and Santa Claus watch over us. They've given me the greatest gift of my life - my little sister will walk, and she'll run! As for me... It takes a while for the tears to subside in any way. Santa Claus says something to my parents, then they both vanish, leaving us to continue crying in the embrace of my older sister and our parents. I've never cried this much in my life, almost howling in relief - because now I'll be able to protect my little sister at school!

"That's enough, my darlings, don't strain yourselves too much," Mum pleads through her tears.

I realize she's crying tears of joy for us. Mum's ecstatic that we're going to walk. And that's even more magical to me than having legs again. After calming down a bit, I hold my youngest sister close, realizing that everything is behind us - the humiliation, the pain, and even the fear of what school might bring. Everything is behind us, and only happiness lies ahead.

"What did Santa Claus say?" I ask amidst my tears.

"He said everyone will think it's how it was from the start," Dad replies, wiping away his tears. "You both had surgery, and now you'll be able to walk. Not right away, but soon."

"Why not right away?" I wonder.

"Your legs need time to adjust," Dad explains, sighing. "They need to be trained, and your hearts need to bear the weight again, you know?"

I understand - we've regained our legs, but they're new, and they don't function on their own. So, we have to learn to walk. And that's what we'll do. But for now, I can stand up, ready to protect my little sister if need be. And Mashenka touches her legs and cries, cries, cries... I understand her perfectly, feeling the sensation return to mine. Feeling the ground beneath my feet, I already long to stand, but I realize it will take time.

"How long?" I ask my dad.

"Two or three months," he sighs. "Maybe sooner, but rushing it wouldn't be wise. Miracles are miracles, but patience is key. At first, you won't be able to walk far, so you'll still need the wheelchairs."

"Two or three months" and "forever" are quite different. I'm prepared to endure it, and so is the youngest, so there's no need to be sad. We should celebrate because now we truly have something worth celebrating, and it's not just New Year's Eve. It's our new legs, our new life, because not being able to walk is incredibly sad. And the youngest cried as she looked at what remained of her legs...

"Now, if you're done with your tears, everyone to the table!" Mum calls out. "We need to rehydrate."

At first, I don't understand her joke, but Alenka explains to me that after crying so much, I should drink more. I listen and nod because I agree. God, I can feel my legs again! I don't know why Ded Moroz decided to help us, but I don't care. The main thing is that everything will be okay now.

We sit at the table, serve salads, and celebrate the New Year. We welcome it with smiles because all the bad times are behind us, and only good times lie ahead. We have a whole year ahead of us, during which we'll learn how Germany differs from our previous home, learn a new language, and learn to walk. We'll make new friends and hopefully avoid making new enemies because we already have enough of those. I just want peace...

YOUNGER

Ded Moroz initially scared my little sister because she thought she was being naughty, but she realized she was actually good, so there was no need to be afraid. She understood and wasn't scared anymore. Then he struck the floor with his stick and... I got legs! I was sitting in my mum's arms and suddenly, there they were - legs! I squealed with joy because... well, legs!

We cried together with our little sister, loudly and openly, but we weren't scolded for it. It was because of our legs! My little sister could already feel her own, which is why we cried together so intensely. Mum, dad, and Alenka hugged us so lovingly and warmly that it made me cry even more because, somehow, I would be able to walk? Daddy definitely persuaded Ded Moroz to give us legs! I know Daddy talked him into it because he can do anything!

After crying, they sat me at the table to eat and drink water, otherwise, I wouldn't have any tears left. Although now, I probably don't want to cry anymore. Suddenly, everything was fine, even better than fine... we ate salads and drank sweet champagne. Baby champagne, but still champagne! And I felt like I was in a dream, unable to fully grasp it all, feeling my legs, wondering if they were real. But they were here, warm, real, and mine! They were weak, but Daddy promised to fix it. I really, truly believed him. But now, I'll probably need help getting dressed too, won't I?

As New Year's Eve came to an end, I yawned, too tired to even eat cake. It felt like something heavy was weighing me down, and I felt a bit scared. Mum reassured me, saying I shouldn't be scared because the evening was very emotional and I was tired. My sister Masha was tired too, from all the crying.

They took us to our room to put us to bed, with Mum, Dad, and Alenka helping us. Mum and big sister helped us change into our pajamas or nightgown, as Mum instructed, which felt like the right thing to do. They changed us separately, taking extra care with my sister, who got scared without her panties. But once she had her trousers on, she calmed down. I wasn't scared because my sister protected me from everything.

Then Daddy takes a seat on a chair and begins to sing. His voice is soothing and gentle, and he sings about birds, dragons, and winged horses. I remember he used to sing to me at bedtime when he lived with us and looked after me. So I quickly drift off to sleep, eager to be in my little sister's arms. I think the fact that we dream about each other is a special gift from Ded Moroz. I'm grateful to him for my legs and for my little sister.

"Are we really going to start walking now?" I ask Masha.

"Yes, gradually," she confirms. "You might still need the wheelchair a bit longer at school, but if anything..."

"Is it the same school as before?" I inquire, feeling a shiver run down my spine at the thought.

"No, Alenka told me," my sister reminds me. "But we don't want to upset you... And we'll be in different classes..."

"I'll be patient," I assure her. "It'll be scary without you, but I'll manage, I promise."

"Everything will be okay," Masha reassures me, patting my hand. "I trust Daddy, and he knows our story."

I trust Daddy too, wholeheartedly. Though I'm very curious about what lies ahead for us, I'll be patient and obedient. I promise, because I have the best family in the world. New Year's Eve turned out to be so enchanting that words can't fully capture its magic. I probably won't be able to describe it.

Then I wake up, greeted by the sight of snow outside the window and the warm sunlight streaming in. A joy fills me in a way I've never felt before. I turn to my little sister and share a smile with her, feeling overwhelmed by the love in her gaze.

We rise from bed, aided by the convenient handles and loops above. As we attempt to change clothes, I encounter a problem—my legs are weak, and I struggle to move them as I want. Pressing a button, I summon Mum into our room.

"Are you both awake?" she asks, beaming at us. "You're such good girls!"

Mum helps us dress, starting with me and then my little sister. Though I could probably manage on my own, she places me in the pram, and we head to freshen up. We brush our teeth to make them sparkle and wash our faces to shake off sleepiness. Then, hand in hand, we venture into the living room, where we spot presents beneath the Christmas tree. But hadn't we already received our biggest gift? It seems there's more excitement in store!

I wheel up to the tree, my older sister places Masha beside me, and then positions us both on the floor. Masha seems hesitant, unsure what to do. I realize she missed New Year's Eve and might not know about presents, so I explain to her that these gifts are for us, with names written on them. I pull a large box toward me—it's labeled "for Masheneka." Inside, I find a dollhouse, beautifully pink and white, brimming with accessories!

The gifts keep coming—gorgeous dresses, a fur-lined coat, toys, and books. My sister also receives stunning clothes, along with a phone featuring a large screen. I, on the other hand, receive a special watch.

"It's a special watch," Alenka explains. "It can track your location and has a button for calling for help or alerting someone if you fall."

"What about my little sister?" I inquire. My older sister smiles, reassuring me that Masha's phone serves the same purpose, equipped with features to summon help if needed.

The gifts are incredible, and they bring tears to our eyes once again. I don't feel envious of Masha's phone because she deserves it. Besides, I don't need a phone when I have Masha by my side. I had one before, in my old life, but it strained my eyes, so I believe it's best to wait. But these presents... They're just so... so...

"Thank you, thank you, thank you, thank you," we chorus to our parents and Alyonka.

It's a New Year's Eve filled with so much happiness that I'll cherish it forever!

WELCOME TO THE SCHOOL

ELDER

Today, we're heading off to school. In Germany, it's the norm - everyone attends school, except under exceptional circumstances, which we don't have. We're in rehab, so we've recovered and are preparing to blend in "like everyone else." It's a bit daunting for me, of course, because I'm uncertain about what will unfold.

Santa Claus aided us with the language. It happened the day after, on the second of January, when my youngest sister suddenly spoke German to our dad. Dad, perhaps out of habit, asked Alenka for something, I don't recall what, and the youngest offered to help her sister. That's when Mom and Dad started questioning both of us, and we realized we had received more gifts than we expected.

That's both good and bad. Good because we won't have to spend a long time studying the language, and bad because we'll have to part ways. Masha is in middle school, and I'm in high school, which are typically separate in Germany. We were upset about it, but Dad mentioned that we should attend an "inclusive" school, where the middle and high schools are separate but adjacent buildings, so we'll still be close to each other. He really understands us well, and I believe he's a magician.

Now it's time for us to head to school. There's no need for uniforms here, so I'm in jeans for comfort, while my little sister opted for a dress, saying it's easier for her to use the toilet that way. Daddy drives us there, encouraging us not to worry, but we hold onto each other tightly and stay quiet. Sis has already gone to her university, Mom is at work, and Dad took the day off because it's our first day at school, and he's nervous.

I don't pay attention to where the car is going, focusing instead on reassuring myself and Mashenka. It's crucial to calm her down because if she's scared, she won't be able to concentrate in class, and Dad assured us that she'll be safe. We're so used to being together that the thought of parting now feels incredibly difficult, almost impossible. But we must, because it's school... So we sit there, embracing each other, while Dad lets out a sigh.

When we arrive at the school parking lot, Dad helps us out and puts us in our strollers. We need to let go, but I can't bring myself to release my little sister, and she starts sobbing. Dad sighs, sitting down beside us. I don't want to leave her side, fearing she might get hurt. She's so small, so vulnerable, like a true angel! I'll be far away, unable to protect her! These thoughts make me cry too.

Suddenly, I hear a friendly male voice asking why the girls are crying. Though it's not threatening, it has a comforting tone. I instinctively move to shield my sister.

"Our younger girls are inseparable," Dad explains calmly. "They just can't bear to be apart."

"I understand," the stranger says, sitting down and turning to me. "Why are you crying?"

"What if something happens to her?" I respond. "She's such a sweet girl..."

"And your younger sister, from what I can see," he observes, "she's afraid of getting hurt... It's not easy... Come with me."

He stands up, motioning for us to follow, but we're too caught up in our tears. Dad attempts to maneuver both my and Mashenka's strollers simultaneously, but it's not working well, so I release my grip on my sister's stroller to manage on my own. After all, we were both invited, so we're not splitting up just yet. I notice a man I don't recognize in the back - short hair, jeans, light jacket, and I think he's wearing glasses. We drive to the primary school building, enter, and arrive at some sort of classroom.

"This is what I suggest," says the stranger, who seems to

hold some authority in the school, judging by the greetings he receives. "The younger girl will go to class, and the older one will wait here and watch through the glass."

I notice that part of the door is made of glass, so I can keep an eye on my sister, and she won't be scared. And neither will I. But what about my lessons? Before I can ask, though, my little sister agrees and heads into the classroom. The teacher promptly helps her settle in, and the other children... they smile at Mashenka, which surprises her.

"What will happen to my lessons?" I inquire quietly.

"You'll miss them today," the man, who turns out to have glasses and a mustache, explains. He has a very kind face. "And tomorrow your little sister will miss hers and sit with you as well. Just make sure you both feel safe and you can focus on your studies. There's a chair for your dad. Did you arrange for an escort?"

"No, we didn't," Dad shakes his head. "But we're the only ones the children trust completely. I might have to fetch my eldest daughter from university."

"The school will assist you," the stranger nods. "Is that acceptable to you?"

"Thank you," I reply quietly, still unsure of who he is and how he managed to resolve everything so smoothly. Well, as long as there are no issues later. "Um..."

"I'm the Rector, my name is Herr Gutmütig, and you're Maria, right?" he smiles at me.

I nod, not fully grasping what "Rector" means. But right

now, what matters most to me is my little sister - how she's settling in, how she looks, how she starts to smile shyly. Mashenka glances at me without getting anxious and joins the lesson. And the teacher... she's engaging with the children! They're in second grade, yet they're playing games, and within minutes, Mashenka is already interacting with them.

"Daddy, what's a 'rector'?" I asked.

"That's what the principal of the school is called in Germany," Daddy smiled at me.

I was simply amazed. This was the principal? This kind, gentle man who found a solution without raising his voice or giving orders, he was the head of the school? The actual principal? It felt like I had stepped into a fairy tale because it was hard for me to imagine such a principal. But now I understood why the teachers were so kind, why there was no shouting or demands for silence... The teacher played with the students, engaged with them, explained things while managing to be everywhere at once, and another teacher came to assist Mashenka... And with no more than fifteen students in the class, why were there two teachers? How could that be?

"There are two of them?" I exclaimed.

"Indeed, my daughter," Daddy nodded. "One teacher alone can't attend to everyone's needs, and your little sister requires extra attention so she doesn't feel sad."

"Sad?" I was at a loss for words.

It seemed like I really was in a fairy tale because that just didn't seem possible. Two teachers who cared about their pupils not feeling... sad?

YOUNGER

It's really hard to be separated from your elder sister, but a kind man, who turned out to be the principal, found a solution. It was like something out of a fairy tale! Usually, principals are strict, but here he was so understanding and gentle.

They lead me into the classroom where I can see my sister and my daddy through the glass, so I feel reassured. The other kids greet me warmly, and then something unexpected happens during the lesson. First of all, the desks are arranged in a circle instead of rows, and the teacher encourages us to switch places, applying what we've just learned. No one minds that I'm in a pram, and another teacher even approaches me to ask if I need anything. Me, in class?!

I'm at a loss for words, but the teacher explains that it's important to speak up if I'm tired, sad, or hungry. She points out a corner where a girl is already resting on cushions, emphasizing that nobody is expected to be a hero or feel bad. It's all so different and overwhelming.

I meet the other girls and boys, and they're all so friendly and diverse. There are no sad faces; everyone seems to enjoy school. It reminds me of Valera, who was often overlooked. I realize that wouldn't happen here. When one girl starts crying because her eyes hurt, her teacher comforts her immediately.

She's not scolded but gently guided to rest, and everyone accepts it without fuss.

After the lesson, I hurry to my little sister to tell her all about it. Meanwhile, the teacher talks to my dad in a calm manner. From what I can hear, she's not complaining but rather praising me, which makes me feel a bit shy.

We're in the middle of recess, but I've decided not to join in because it takes too long to get ready. Instead, I'm sitting with my little sister. Surprisingly, nobody bothers us. It's quite unusual for me, actually very unusual. During lessons, my sister keeps a close eye on me to ensure I'm not mistreated, but everyone around us is really kind, so I don't feel worried. Still, I want to make sure my sister feels comfortable, so we decide to visit her classroom.

She's scared... I can tell just by looking at her, so I give her a hug. Dad comforts us both, but when it's time to enter the classroom, my sister hesitates, glancing back at Dad, and I can see she's on the verge of tears. I'm not sure what's wrong, but I stroke her gently to reassure her, and Dad doesn't push it either.

"Why don't I come with you?" I suggest to my little sister. "Or Dad?"

"What's the matter?" asks the teacher, who must be the uncle mentioned earlier.

"My daughter had a rough time at her old school," Dad explains to him. "She's afraid of being bullied, even if it's subconscious."

"I see..." the teacher says thoughtfully, then heads into the classroom, calling someone out.

After a short while, older students emerge from the classroom. They introduce themselves and assure her that she's safe because she's a good girl. My sister asks why they think so, and they explain that it's just obvious. Surprised but relieved, she agrees to go with them, and they lead her away while I stay with Dad, waiting for her.

The older students have different lessons from ours, but they're just as interesting, maybe even more so. My sister quickly forgets her fears, engaging in conversation and activities with her new classmates.

"Dad," I ask as we wait, "what happened to that... um, grandfather... well..."

"Oh, my dear," Dad sighs. "He packed up and discarded all the belongings, both mine and yours, then punished himself."

"How come?" I inquire, not fully grasping Dad's explanation.

"You're a German citizen," Dad explains. "Legally, your belongings can't be taken away from you by someone who isn't your guardian or legal representative. That's why your grandfather ended up in prison. For stealing."

"Oh," I can't help but say. It's a shame, of course, about all my dresses and toys, but I'll still have them. What I do like is knowing that the grandfather who betrayed me is in prison. I like that a lot, even though I didn't witness the moment he abandoned me. I understand it all now. My little sister even shielded me from that. She's truly, truly good.

After school, we head home to have a discussion. We need to figure out our next steps. My little sister is very scared, but I believe she's protected, and I'm not upset. It feels like we can handle things on our own now, like we're living in a fairy tale. Everything around us seems too good to be true.

"Why are we not going home?" I ask, noticing we're going in a different direction.

"To the hospital, dear," Daddy says gently. "You're in rehab, you need to exercise."

I had forgotten! We go to the hospital every day, where Daddy takes us. If he's at work, then Mom or my sister takes us, or the hospital minibus comes to pick us up. We do crawling exercises, preparing to start walking soon. It looks like we're recovering faster than Daddy expected, and even faster than the doctors anticipated.

It feels like all the bad times are behind us, and we have a very happy life ahead. We have Alyonka, Mom, and Dad. We'll soon be out of the prams, so everything will be fine. Daddy says if it can't be otherwise, there's no need to worry.

By the end of her lesson, my sister was smiling. I could tell she was fortunate and no one tried to bully her, as she feared. For some reason, the other students turned out to be very kind. I wonder if we're just lucky or if it will always be like this. I ask Daddy and learn that bullying does happen in Germany, but it leads to serious consequences. Even the police get involved. Back where we're from, what my sister did when she misbehaved wouldn't have just resulted in a slap on the wrist; she would have gone to prison. But in Germany, hitting children on the behind is forbidden altogether.

It feels like we're in a fairy tale.

FLOW OF TIME

ELDER

This could only happen to me! Just yesterday, I was skating down the hill with my youngest, and now here I am, all twisted up and unable to straighten out... Naturally, I get scared at first. It always hits me first. So, I get scared, then my sister gets scared, and she calls for Dad.

"Daddy! Masha's sick!" she screams as soon as she sees me, barely managing to crawl to the bed.

It took us a month to recover. It was a really tough month, and if it weren't for Mom, Dad, and Alyonka, I don't know what would've happened. But we made it through. And our youngest, my little angel, she made it too! We made progress step by step, quite literally. Sometimes it was unbearable because her legs couldn't handle the strain, and she cried a lot. Well, I cried too.

Then came my first time, and it wasn't pleasant at all, just as Dad had warned. Menstrual periods are excruciatingly painful for me, to the point of fainting. Only a special pill helps, but the sensation is like being impaled right on that spot. Dad explained it's because I was frequently and harshly hit with a belt in childhood. He said it should get easier after the first birth. You need love to give birth, and I'm afraid of boys, so I don't know...

Dad comes in, gives me a pill, and then I just lie there, quietly whimpering. I'm in such a whimpering mood. And to top it off, we only planned to stay here for three days, but it's been five days now. It's so frustrating, I can't believe it! And I've ruined my little one's fun because she won't have fun if her sister's not happy. She's my miracle... Such a magical girl. We all adore her, especially me.

As I lie there quietly whimpering, my mind wanders. It's been two months since I started school. My classmates, or "colleagues" as they're called here, have been so supportive of every little achievement of mine that they feel like siblings... And the same goes for my little sister. When she showed up without her pram for the first time, her class threw a big celebration, and no one made a fuss about it.

We still dream of each other, so it feels like we're never really apart, except during school hours. But we're not afraid for each other anymore, because everyone around us is so kind. In the family, to avoid confusion, we're simply referred to as Elder and Younger. Alyonka doesn't mind being called Younger, even though she's the oldest in our family. She says it's even better that way.

"Well, the eldest isn't feeling well," Dad tactfully informs the rest of the family. "Younger isn't going anywhere without her. So, anyone up for the slide?"

"That's a silly question, Daddy," Alyonka says with a smile. "It's obvious we won't go anywhere without the younger ones. Let's head home."

I might have cried about this before, but now I don't. I've grown accustomed to it – we're a united family, a whole, and we refuse to be apart from each other. Even though Alyonka came for a special outing, she won't go without us. So Dad nods and heads downstairs to check out and fetch the car. I feel a bit embarrassed, but not too much, because Dad says it's normal to support each other. So I try not to worry too much, though there's still a bit of a knot in my stomach...

Mom starts getting ready, showing no signs of displeasure, and neither does Alenka. Our eldest sister sits beside me, gently comforting both me and our little one. She's upset because she thinks everyone's leaving because of her, but Alenka understands and soothes Mashenka.

Dad's bringing the car around, and soon we'll be heading home. We'll be staying home for a couple of days, although the little one will probably go to the playground. And then it's my birthday. It's never been celebrated before. I... I'm yearning for something magical, I want a miracle! So what if I'm fourteen! Oh, I'll be fifteen... I'll be fifteen, but I want it to feel like I'm a little girl again – with dolls, a table full of sweets...

In my daydreams, I forget that my youngest sister knows everything, just like my dreams do. Of course, she shares everything with our parents. So time passes, my stomach settles, and one morning... I'm excused from school without knowing why, and then the alarm clock starts playing "happy birthday to you" right from the morning, so I don't wake up immediately. My little sister jumps on me first, and then the whole family starts congratulating me while I'm still in bed.

Dad picks me up in his arms, even though I'm long and heavy, but I feel so snug in his embrace that I don't even think about resisting. I'm bathed like a little girl, and then they seat me at the table in my pajamas. Mom looks at me with a mischievous twinkle in her eyes and asks me to open my mouth. Even though I'm an adult now, it's as if they've read all my secret desires, ones I haven't even shared with my sister!

I'm spoon-fed, showered with gifts, hugged, dressed, and not allowed to do anything by myself. This would have scared me a year ago, but now I feel so warm, so content, so extraordinary that it's indescribable.

"And school?" I inquire.

"You're both off from school today, sister," Masha informs me. "We're going for a surprise!"

"What kind of surprise?" I ask, already sensing there won't be an answer.

I get into the car, Alenka, who's come especially for my birthday, adjusts the baby seat for the youngest one, so I'm sandwiched between my sisters, and then the car starts moving. I'm so caught up in the conversation and hugs that I don't notice where we're headed. Three hours pass by unnoticed, and then...

It's my childhood dream. I once saw a report about this park on TV, and since then, I've been dreaming of visiting it at least once. I knew it was impossible, just a magical fantasy, like a flying carpet or journeying far away, where nobody knows me, where I don't have to fight for my place in the sun...

Magnificent roller coasters reaching for the sky. Thrilling loops that take your breath away. Swings, carousels, pirate ships... and a small children's train that I somehow manage to fit into. And above all this grandeur, a monorail gliding gracefully. I squeal with delight like a little girl, laughing and crying tears of joy. Finally, I fully accept that I am not Mad Mashka anymore, but... Elder. Never again will I be that troubled girl who haunts my nightmares, causing me to wake up screaming and crying.

Surrounded by my family, I am the happiest girl in the world. The happiest, because this is something I never even dared to dream of before, not so long ago. I have the best little sister I could have ever wished for... The best family... The best life. The nightmare is behind me now, and I can face the future with a smile, basking in the warmth of the sun. I wonder if I will succeed in all that I have planned.

YOUNGER

I sit outside the gymnasium, clenching my fists. When my little sister started attending gymnasium, I decided to join too. After all, she's my sister, and having two Mashas with the same surname amused the teachers. Nearly five years have flown by, and now my little sister is taking her final exams, gearing up to earn her "abitur" and gain entry to university. Without it, they won't even consider her application, so these exams hold immense importance.

It feels like just yesterday, yet it feels like a lifetime ago. I comprehend so much more now, especially what eluded me back then. My little sister is a saint. Despite any past missteps, she's my guardian angel, shielding me from the darkest of times for six months. She shared her warmth, a warmth she didn't even know she possessed. And even before that... Now I understand where biopapa intended to go one day, and where biomama ended up. I use those terms because my dad and mom are the epitome of goodness. Dad would never dream of having a beer while driving, and Mom wouldn't dare to distract him in the car. It's just basic rules!

I've learned that "there" was a whole network of despicable individuals, all of whom wound up behind bars due to an international scandal. Even if there hadn't been a New Year's miracle, I would have eventually walked with the help of special prosthetics. Yes, it would have been tougher, but with this family, anything is possible. Santa Claus restored my childhood, for it's not about legs—it's about miracles!

My older sister has chosen to become a teacher for children. She'll be heading to university to enlighten kids about the importance of being good. That's her essence—explaining, aiding, consoling, warming hearts.

Alenka tied the knot a year ago. She's blessed with a wonderful partner and their love mirrors that of our parents. They set the bar high for us all, being the most enchanting parents in the world! Eldest also has a boyfriend, but they're taking it slow as she prioritizes her studies. She's a determined little sister, that's for sure!

"Sis!" Elder called out, and I hurried over to her.

I can see pure joy on her face, as she's drawing closer to her dreams. Our parents and Alyonka, who's carrying a baby bump not yet visible, fill her with excitement. Alyonka will undoubtedly be an exceptional mom, I just know it! And one day, I'll follow suit... When I head off to university, my little sister will already have her diploma, yet we'll still rendezvous in our dreams, ensuring we're never apart. Isn't that how it should be?

"Well, everyone's passed everything, the year's wrapped up, shall we go?" Dad inquires.

"Yeah! Hooray!" We leap about, despite being all grown up. "To the sea!"

It's a special treat for us—a whole month by the sea. A month of beaches, water parks, and boat trips. And... and... and... and... and... And we'll fly there together by plane! That's the plan.

That's the gist of it. We relish this month-long vacation before returning to our studies. I have the most wonderful classmates! While my sister isn't overly fond of her university group, we persevere. Sometimes it's tough, but I've got a "trick" up my sleeve—my sister explains things to me in my dreams, helping me grasp concepts faster than others. That's why I consistently excel—earning high marks on my certificates. Our parents beam with pride, their words lifting me up, because it's truly, truly...

I understand very clearly that without my sister, I wouldn't be here today. She's the reason I survived the harshness of children's shelter and regular school. She shielded me from harm and kept me whole. Sometimes I even dream about being separated, though my sister and I share more than just dreams where we're always together. I don't dwell on why it happens; I simply let things unfold as they will...

Years have passed, and now I, Elder, am a young teacher. Yet here I sit on the same bench beside my aging parents, my fists clenched with excitement. I sneak up on them, ready to unleash a happy shriek. My dream is to become a doctor—

ever since Daddy witnessed me and my sister undergo a botched operation. I want to be just like Daddy.

"Vee-ee-ee-ee-ee!" I squeal, while my little sister, who's long spotted me, startles me playfully, and Alenka, cradling her little one, offers a warm smile.

Mom and Dad are overjoyed for me, and I'm confident that everything will always be alright. My boyfriend arrives with a bouquet of flowers... He knows my favorite blooms, and he became serious after talking to my older sister. She grilled him so thoroughly I feared he'd leave, but he stayed, acting like a proper gentleman. She truly is magic. And she has me, of course! What more could one ask for?

The tale of the mischievous little girl and her angelic sister comes to a close. It was a challenging journey, even with Santa Claus performing his miracles, but perhaps the crux of the story isn't that. It's about the warmth of family—the people who understand and embrace whatever comes their way. Good doesn't always birth good, but evil invariably begets evil, prompting the girl to feel vulnerable in order to transform. With the help of Santa's helpers, a whole family found happiness, saving many lives in the process.

In a distant land, officials pondered, marking a victory of sorts. And the two Mashas lived out their dreams, basking in their newfound happiness. Their wishes had come true. May all the bright, magical dreams of children come to fruition. May they smile and revel in each new day. May it always be so.

www.ingramcontent.com/pod-product-compliance
Lightning Source LLC
LaVergne TN
LVHW011933070526
838202LV00054B/4623